# TROIKA

# TROIKA

## ALASTAIR REYNOLDS

SUBTERRANEAN PRESS • 2011

**First Edition**

**ISBN**
978-1-59606-376-1

Subterranean Press
PO Box 190106
Burton, MI 48519

www.subterraneanpress.com

B
Y THE TIME I reach the road to Zvezdniy Gorodok acute hypothermia is beginning to set in. I recognise the symptoms from my training: stage one moving into two, as my body redirects blood away from skin to conserve heat—shivering and a general loss of coordination the result. Later I can expect a deterioration of vasomotor tone as the muscles now contracting my peripheral blood vessels become exhausted. As blood surges back to my chilled extremities, I'll start to feel hot rather than cold. Slipping ever further into disorientation, it will take an effort of will not to succumb to that familiar and distressing syndrome, paradoxical undressing. The few layers of clothes I'm wearing—the pyjamas, the thin coat I stole from Doctor Kizim—will start feeling too warm. They'll find me naked and dead in the snow.

How long have I been out? An hour, two hours? There's no way to tell. It's like being back on the *Tereshkova*, when we slept so little that a day could feel like a week. All I know is that it's still night. When the sun is up it will be harder to move around, but until then there's still time to locate Nesha Petrova.

I touch the metal prize in my pocket, reassuring myself that it's still there.

As if invoked by the act of touching the prize, a monstrous machine roars toward me out of the night. It's yellow, with an angled shovel on the front. I stumble into the path of its headlights and raise a wary hand. The snowplough sounds its horn. I jerk back, avoiding the blade and the flurry of dirty snow it flings aside.

I think for a moment it's going to surge on past. Instead the machine slows and stops. Maybe he thinks he's hit me. It's good—a robot snowplough wouldn't stop, so there must be someone operating this one. I hobble around to the cab, where the driver's glaring at me through an unopened window. He's got a moustache, a woollen hat jammed down over his hair and ears, the red nose of a serious drinker.

Above the snorting, impatient diesel I call: 'I could use a ride to town.'

The driver looks at me like I'm dirt, some piece of roadside debris he'd have been better shovelling into the verge. This far out of town, on this road, it doesn't take much guesswork to figure out where I've come from. The hospital, the facility, the madhouse, whatever you want to call it, will have been visible in the distance on a clear day—a forbidding smudge of dark, tiny-windowed buildings, tucked behind high, razor-topped security fencing.

He lowers the window an inch. 'Do yourself a favour, friend. Go back, get warm.'

'I won't make it back. Early-onset hypothermia. Please, take me to Zvezdniy Gorodok. I can't give you much, but you're welcome to these.' My fingers feel like awkward tele-operated waldos, the kind we'd had on the Progress. I fumble a pack of cigarettes from my coat pocket and push the crushed and soggy rectangle up to the slit in the window.

'All you've got?'

'They're American.'

The driver grunts something unintelligible, but takes the cigarettes anyway. He opens the pack to inspect the contents, sniffing at them. 'How old are these?'

'You can still smoke them.'

The driver leans over to open the other door. 'Get in. I'll take you as far as the first crossroads on the edge of town. You get out when we stop. You're on your own from then on.'

I'll agree to any arrangement provided it gets me a few minutes in the warmth of the cab. For now I'm still lucid enough to recognise the hypothermia creep-ing over me. That state of clinical detachment won't last forever.

I climb in, taking deep, shivering breaths.

'Thank you.'

'The edge of town, that's as far as we go,' he says, as if I didn't get it the first time. His breath stinks of alcohol. 'I'm caught giving you a ride, it won't be good for me.'

'I doubt it'll be good for either of us.'

The driver shifts the snowplough back into gear and lets her roll, the engine bellowing as the blade bites snow. 'They'll find you in Zvezdniy Gorodok. It's not that big a place. It's the arse end of nowhere and the trains aren't running.'

'I only need to get to town.'

He looks at me, assessing the shabbiness of my dress, the state of my beard and hair. 'Wild night ahead of you?'

'Something like that.'

He's got the radio on, tuned to the state classical music channel. It's playing Prokofiev. I lean over and turn the volume down, until it's almost lost under the engine noise.

'I was listening to that.'

'Please. Until we get there.'

'Got a problem with music?'

'Some of it.'

The driver shrugs—he doesn't seem to mind as much as he pretends. Panicking suddenly, imagining I might have dropped it in the snow, I pat my pocket again. But—along with Doctor Kizim's security pass—the little metal box is still there.

It takes all of my resolve not to take it out and turn the little handle that makes it play. Not because I can stand to hear it again, but because I want to be sure it still works.

ᘒᘒ

The snowplough's taillights fade into the night. The driver has kept to his word, taking us through the abandoned checkpoint, then to the first crossroads inside the old city boundary and no further. It's been good to get warm, my clothes beginning to dry, but now that I'm outside again the cold only takes a few seconds to reach my bones. The blizzard has abated while we drove, but the snow's still falling, coming down in soft flurries from a milky predawn sky.

At this early hour Zvezdniy Gorodok gives every indication of being deserted. The housing blocks are mostly unlit, save for the occasional illuminated window—a pale, curtained rectangle of dim yellow against the otherwise dark edifice. The buildings, set back from the intersecting roads in long ranks, look drearily similar, as if stamped from the same machine tool—even the party images flickering on their sides are the same from building to building. The same faces, the same slogans. For a moment I have the sense of having embarked on a ludicrous and faintly delusional task. Any one of these buildings could be where she lives. They'll find me long before I have time to search each lobby, hoping to find a name.

I'd shown the driver the address I'd written down, pulled from the public telephone directory on Doctor Kizim's desk. He'd given me a rough idea of where I ought to head. The apartment complex is somewhere near the railway station—I'll have to search the surrounding streets until I find it.

'I know where the station is,' I tell the driver. 'I was here when it was a sealed training facility.'

'You had something to do with the space program?'

'I did my bit.'

Zvezdniy Gorodok—Starry Town, or Star City. In the old days, you needed a permit just to get into it. Now that the space program is over—it has "achieved all necessary objectives", according to the official line of the Second Soviet—Zvezdniy Gorodok is just another place to live, work and die. Utilitarian housing projects radiate far beyond the old boundary. The checkpoint is a disused ruin and the labs and training facilities have been turned into austere community buildings. More farmers and factory workers live here now than engineers, scientists and former cosmonauts.

I'm lucky to have got this far.

I escaped through a gap in the facility's security fence, in a neglected corner of the establishment tucked away behind one of the kitchens. I'd known about the breech for at least six months—long enough to reassure myself that no one else had noticed it, and that the break could not be seen from the administrative offices or any of the surveillance cameras. It was good fortune that the gap existed, but I still wouldn't have got far without the help from Doctor Kizim. I don't know if he expects me to succeed in my escape attempt, but Doctor Kizim—who had always been more sympathetic to the *Tereshkova*'s survivors than any of the other medics—did turn a conveniently blind eye. It was his coat that I had taken. Not much good against blizzards, but without it I'd never have got as far as the snowplough, let alone Zvezdniy Gorodok. I just hope he doesn't get into too much trouble when they find out I took it.

I don't expect to get the chance to apologise to him.

The snow's stopped falling, and a pink frigid sun is trying to break through the gloom on the eastern horizon. I locate the railway station, and begin to explore the surrounding streets, certain I can't be wrong. More lights have come on now and I'm noticing the stirrings of daily activity. One or two citizens pass me in the snow, but they have their heads down and pay me little heed. Few vehicles are on the roads, and with the trains not running the area around the station is almost totally devoid of activity. When a large car—a Zil limousine, black and muscular as a panther—swings onto the street I'm walking down, I don't have time to hide. But the Zil sails by, tyres spraying muddy slush, and as it passes I see that it's empty. The car must be on its way to collect a party official from one of the better districts.

I've been walking for an hour, trying not to glance over my shoulder too often, when I find Nesha's building.

The apartment complex has a public entrance lobby smelling of toilets and alcohol. Plywood panels cover some of the windows in the outer wall, where the glass has broken. It's draughty and unlit, the tiled floor filthy with footprints and paper and smashed glass. The door into the rest of the building can only be opened by someone inside. In my cold, sodden slippers I squelch to the buzzer panel next to the mailboxes.

I catch my breath. Everything hinges on this moment. If I'm wrong about Nesha, or if she's moved elsewhere, or died—it's been a long time, after all—then everything, everything, will have been for nothing.

But her name's still there.

*N. Petrova.* She lives on the ninth floor.

It may mean nothing. She may still have died or been moved on. I reach out a numb finger and press the buzzer anyway. There's no sound, no reassuring response. I wait a minute then press it again. Outside, a stray dog with mad eyes yellows the snow under a lamp-post. I press the buzzer again, shivering more than when I was outside.

A woman's voice crackles through the grille above the buzzers. 'Yes?'

'Nesha Petrova?' I ask, leaning to bring my lips closer to the grille.

'Who is it?'

'Dimitri Ivanov.' I wait a second or two for her to respond to the name.

'From building services?'

I assume that there's no camera letting Nesha see me, if there ever was. 'Dimitri Ivanov, the cosmonaut. I was on the ship, the *Tereshkova*. The one that met the Matryoshka.'

Silence follows. I realise, dimly, that there's an eventuality I've never allowed for. Nesha Petrova may be too old to remember anything of importance. She may be too old to care.

I shuffle wet feet to stave off the cold.

'Nesha?'

'There were three cosmonauts.'

I lean into the grille again. 'The other two were Galenka Makarova and Yakov Demin. They're both dead now. The VASIMIR engine malfunctioned on the way home, exposing them to too much radiation. I'm the only one left.'

'Why should I believe you?'

'Because I'm standing here in pyjamas and a stolen coat. Because I've come all the way from the facility just to see you, through the snow. Because there's something I want you to know.'

'Then tell me.'

'I'd rather show you. Besides, I'm going to die of cold if I stand here much longer.'

I look to the outside world again, through one of the panes that hasn't been broken and covered over with plywood. Another Zil slides by. This one has bodies in it: grey-skinned men sitting upright in dark coats and hats.

'I don't want any trouble from the police.'

'I won't stay long. Then I'll be on my way, and no one will have to know that I was here.'

'I'll know.'

'Please, let me in.' I haven't bargained for this. In all the versions of this encounter that I've run through my mind before the escape, she never needed any persuasion to meet me. 'Nesha, you need to understand. They tried to bury you, but you were right all along. That's what I want to tell you about. Before they silence me, and no one ever gets to find out.'

After an age she says: 'You think it matters now, Dimitri Ivanov? You think anything matters?'

'More than you can imagine,' I say.

The door buzzes. She's letting me in.

⟵⟶

'It's blacker than I was expecting.'

I paused in my hamfisted typing. 'Of course it's black. What other colour were you expecting?'

Yakov was still staring out the porthole, at the looming Matryoshka. It was two hundred kilometres away, but still ate up more than half the sky. No stars in that direction, just a big absence like the mother of all galactic supervoids. We had the cabin lights dimmed so he could get a good view. We had already spread the relay microsats around the alien machine, ready for when the Progress penetrated one of the transient windows in Shell 3. But you couldn't see the microsats from here—they were tiny, and the machine was vast.

'What I mean is ...' Yakov started saying.

'Is that it's black.'

'I mean it's more than black. It's like—black was black, and now there's something in my head that's even darker, like a colour I never imagined until now. But which was always there, just waiting for this moment.'

'I'm concerned about you, comrade,' said Galenka, who was riding the exercise cycle in one corner of the module. She was wearing a skin-tight load-suit, designed to preserve muscle tone even in weightlessness. Maybe I'd been in space too long, but she looked better in that load-suit every day.

'You don't feel it, then?' Yakov asked, directing his question to both of us.

'It's just dark,' I said. 'I guess nothing's really prepared us for this, but it's not something we should be surprised about. The last two apparitions ...'

'Just machines, just dumb space probes. This is the first time anyone's seen it with their own eyes.' Yakov turned slowly from the porthole. He was pale, with the puffy, slit-eyed look we'd all developed since leaving Earth. 'Don't you think that changes things? Don't you think us being out here, us being observers, changes things? We're not just making measurements on this thing from a distance now. We're interacting, touching it, feeling it.'

'And I think you need to get some sleep,' Galenka said.

I folded the workstation keyboard back into its recess. I had been answering questions from schoolchildren; the selected few that had been deemed worthy of my attention by the mission schedulers.

'Tell me you don't feel a little freaked out, Dimitri.'

'Maybe a bit,' I allowed. 'But no more than I'd feel if we were in orbit around Mars, or Venus, or creeping up on an asteroid. It's a very big thing and we're very small and a long way from home.'

'This is also a very alien big thing. It was made by alien minds, for a purpose we can't grasp. It's not just some lump of rock with a gravitational field. It's a machine, a ship, that they sent to our solar system for a reason.'

'It's a dead alien thing,' Galenka said, huffing as she cycled harder, pushing through an uphill part of her training schedule. 'Someone made it once, but it's broken now. Fucked like an old clock. If it wasn't fucked, it wouldn't be on this stupid elliptical orbit.'

'Maybe this orbit is all part of the plan,' Yakov said.

'He's starting to sound like Nesha Petrova,' Galenka said teasingly. 'Be careful, Yakov. You know what happened to her when she didn't shut up with her silly ideas.'

'What plan?' I asked.

'That thing must be thousands of years old. Tens of thousand, maybe more. The fact that it's been on this orbit for twenty-four years proves nothing. It's an eye-blink, as far as that thing's concerned. It might just be waking up, running systems checks, rebooting itself. It came through a wormhole. Who knows what that does to something?'

'You certainly don't,' Galenka said.

'She's right,' I said. 'It's dead. If it was going to wake up, it would have done so during the first two apparitions. We poked and prodded it enough the second time; nothing happened.'

'I wish I shared your reassurance.'

I shrugged. 'We're just here to do a job, Yakov. Get in, get out. Then go home and get the glory, like good cosmonauts. Before I worried about the Matryoshka, I'd worry about not screwing up your part in it.'

'I'm not going to screw up.' He looked at me earnestly, as if I had challenged him. 'Did I ever screw up in the simulations, Dimitri? Did I ever screw up once?'

'No,' I admitted. 'But this isn't a simulation. We're not in Star City now.'

He winked at me. 'Absolutely sure of that, comrade?'

⊖⊖

I wiped the sleeve of my load-suit against the portal glass to clear the condensation. From around the curve of the ship there was a puff of silvery brightness as the pyrotechnic docking latches released their hold on the Progress. In the same instant I heard a faraway thud and felt the fabric of the ship lurch with the recoil.

'Confirm separation,' Yakov reported, calling from another porthole. 'Looks like a clean birth to me, boys and girls.'

Galenka was webbed into a hammock at the Progress workstation, one hand on a joystick and the other tapping a keyboard. The screens before her were alive with camera views, from both the *Tereshkova* and the little robot that had just detached from it.

'Beginning thruster translation,' she said, touching keys. 'You should see her in a few seconds, Dimitri.'

The Progress drifted over my horizon, a pea-green shuttlecock with CCCP stencilled down the side in red letters. Very slowly it pulled away from the *Tereshkova* and tipped around on two axes, pointing its nose at the forbidding darkness of the Matryoshka. 'Looking good,' I said, inspecting every visible inch of the space-craft for signs of damage. 'No impacts that I can see. Looks as good as the day they wheeled her out of the clean room.'

'Stirring hydrazine tanks,' Galenka said. 'Let's see if she holds, shall we?'

'Still there,' I reported, when the Progress had failed to blow itself apart. 'Looks like we have a viable spacecraft. Shall I break out the vodka?'

'Let's not get ahead of ourselves—no use going in if we're blind. Beginning camera and waldo deployment—this'll be the real test.'

Our little envoy looked like a cross between a spaceship and a deep-sea submersible robot, the kind they use to explore shipwrecks and pull missiles out of sunken submarines. Arms and sensors and cameras had been bolted onto the front, ruining whatever vague aerodynamics the Progress might have had. Now the equipment—stowed since launch—was slowly deploying, like a flower opening to the sun. Galenka pushed aside the joystick and tugged down a set of waldo controls, slipping her fingers into the heavy, sensor-laden gloves and sleeves. Out in space, the Progress's mechanical arms and hands echoed her gestures. It looked good to me but Galenka still frowned and made some small adjustments to the settings. Ever the perfectionist, I thought. More check-out tests followed until she signified grudging satisfaction.

'Camera assembly three is a little stiff—I wouldn't be surprised if it seizes on us mid-mission. Haptic feedback on arm two is delayed just enough to throw me off. We've lost a row of pixels on the mid infrared array—probably a bad cosmic ray strike. I'm already reading an event overflow in one of the memory buffers, and we haven't even started logging data.'

'But you're happy to continue?' I asked.

'Unless we brought a second Progress no one told me about, we're stuck with this one.'

'It's nothing we can repair,' Yakov said. 'So we may as well live with it. Even if we went out in the suits, we don't have the tools to fix those instruments.'

'I don't need that spelled out,' Galenka said, just barely keeping a lid on her temper.

Yakov was starting to needle both of us. The Matryoshka was getting to him in a way it wasn't yet getting to Galenka, or me for that matter. He'd started coming out with some very odd statements. The joke of his, that we were still back in Star City, that all of this was an elaborate simulation, a preparation for the mission to come—even down to the impossible-to-fake weightlessness—was beginning to wear thin.

What bothered me was that I wasn't even sure he was joking any more.

People cracked in space. It was part of the job. That was why we had duct-tape and tasers aboard. I just hadn't expected it to happen to one of us, so soon in the mission. We hadn't even touched the Matryoshka yet. What was going to happen when the Progress reached the secret layers beneath Shell 3?

I tried not to think about it.

⋐⋑

'What's your approach speed?' I asked, looming behind Galenka while she worked the controls.

'Two metres per second, on the nail.'

'A little on the fast side, aren't we?'

Galenka touched a hand over the mike, so Baikonur wouldn't hear what she had to say next. 'You flying this thing, or me, comrade?'

'You are, definitely.' I scratched at chin stubble. 'It's just that I thought we were going to keep it below one meter a second, all the way in.'

'You want to sit around for thirty hours, be my guest.'

'I wouldn't be the one doing the sitting.'

'This is well within acceptable limits. We'll make up speed in the gaps and slow down when we hit anything knotty. Trust me on this, all right?'

'You're the pilot.'

'That's the general idea.'

She un-cupped the microphone. 'Holding approach speed, Baikonur. Progress systems stable. One hundred meters into Shell 1. Predictive impact model still holding. No change in the status of the Matryoshka or the surrounding vacuum.'

On the screen, wireframe graphics traced the vast right-angled shapes of radar-illuminated obstacles— iceberg or battle-cruiser sized slabs of inscrutably dark free-flying machinery, between which the Progress was obliged to navigate a path, avoiding not only the obstacles but the invisible threads of razor-thin force binding them together. Shell 1 was not a solid sphere, but a swarm of deadly obstacles and tripwires.

During the second apparition, the Americans had sent one of their robot probes straight through one of those field threads. It had gone instantly silent, suggesting that it had suffered a fatal or damaging collision. Years later, deep space radar had picked it up drifting powerless on a sun-circling orbit. A manned expedition (one of the last the Americans ever managed) was sent out to recover it and bring it back to Earth for inspection.

Yet when the astronauts got hold of part of the probe, an entire half of it drifted silently away from the other, separating along a mathematically perfect plane of bisection. The astronauts stared in mute incomprehension at the sliced-through interior of the robot, its tight-packed, labyrinthine innards gleaming back at them with the polish of chrome. The robot must have been cut in two as it passed through the Matryoshka, but so cleanly that the two parts had continued moving on exactly the same trajectory, until this moment.

Although it was only the robot we were sending in, with the *Tereshkova* parked at a safe distance, I still shuddered to think what those lines of force could do to metal and ceramic, to flesh and bone. The predictive model traced the vectors of the field lines and offered solutions for safe passage, but, try as I might, I couldn't share Galenka's unflappable faith in the power of algorithm and computer speed.

Still, like she said, she was the pilot. This was her turf and I was well advised not to trample on it. I'd have felt exactly the same way if she had dared tell me how to manage the *Tereshkova*'s data acquisition and transmission systems.

Following a plan that had been argued over for months back on Earth, it had been agreed to attempt sample collection at each stage of the Progress's journey. The predictive model gave us confidence that the robot could get close to one of the free-flying obstacles without being sliced by the field lines. Dropping the Progress's speed to less than a meter per second, Galenka brought it within contact range of a particular lump of alien machinery and extended the arms and analysis tools to their full extent. Thanks to a Chinese probe that had gone off-course during the second apparition, we knew that the outer integument was surprisingly brittle. The probe had destroyed itself utterly in its high-velocity collision, but not before chipping off vast chunks of alien material. To our delight, early surveys of the Matryoshka on its third return had shown that the impacted obstacle had not repaired itself.

The Progress anchored itself by firing sticky-tipped guy-lines onto the obstacle. Galenka used hammers, cutting devices and claws to pick away at the scabbed edge of the impact point. Pieces of integument flaked away easily—had we been out there in our EVA suits, we could have ripped them out by hand. Some of them were coal-sized, some were as large as engine blocks. Galenka loaded up a third of the Progress's cargo space before deeming the haul sufficient. She wanted room for more samples when she got further in.

'Want to bring her back, unload and return?' I asked. The plan had been to make multiple forays into the Matryoshka, until we'd exhausted our hydrazine reserves.

'Not with the systems as screwed as they are. We lose camera rotation, or blow some more memory, we're blind. Maybe we'll get three or four missions out of the robot, but right now I'm assuming this is our one chance. I'd like to go deeper, at least until we have a full hold.'

'You want to consult with Baikonur?'

'We have discretion here, Dimitri. Timelag's too great to go crying to mummy every time we have a decision to make.' She withdrew her hands from the waldo controls and flexed her fingers. 'I'm taking her further in, while we still have a ship that works.'

'I'm fine with that.'

'Good,' she said, massively indifferent to whether I was "fine" with it or not. Then: 'Where's Yakov right now, by the way?'

'Somewhere.'

'One of us needs to keep an eye on him, Dimitri. Not happy with that guy. I think he's on the edge.'

'We're all on the edge. It's called being in space.'

'I'm just saying.'

'Keep an eye on him, yes. I will.'

At fifteen kilometres, the Progress cleared Shell 1 and passed into a volume of open space largely devoid of moving obstacles or field lines. Galenka notched up the speed, until the Progress was falling inwards at a kilometre every ten seconds. There was nothing here to sample or analyse. 'Normal vacuum in Gap 1,' she murmured. 'Or at least what the robot reads as normal. The ambient physics hasn't changed too much.'

Ever since the first apparition, it had been known—or at least suspected—that the Matryoshka was not just a mysteriously layered artefact drifting through space.

In some way that we didn't yet understand, the object distorted the very physics of the spacetime in which it was floating. The effects were almost too subtle to measure at the distance of the *Tereshkova*, but they became more severe the closer any probes got to the middle. Fundamental constants stopped being fundamental. The speed of light varied. Planck's constant deviated from the figure in textbooks. So did the weak mixing angle, the fine-structure constant, Newton's constant. None of this could be explained under any existing theory of physics. It was as if the Matryoshka was dragging a chunk of another universe around with it. Perhaps it had been designed that way, or perhaps the altered spacetime was a kind of lingering contamination, a side-effect of wormhole travel.

Of course, we didn't know for sure that the Matryoshka had come through a wormhole. That was just an educated guess papered over the vast, yawning chasm of our ignorance. All we knew for sure was that it had appeared, accompanied by a flash of energy, in the middle of the solar system.

I remembered that day very well. November the sixth, twenty fifteen. My twentieth birthday, to the day. Twenty four years later—two of the Matryoshka's looping, twelve year elliptical orbits around the Sun—and here I was, staring the thing in the face, as if my whole adult life had been an arrow pointing to this moment.

Maybe it had.

I was born in ninety ninety five, in Klushino. It's a small place near Smolensk. It wouldn't have any claim to fame except Klushino is the place where Yuri Gagarin was born. I knew that name almost before I knew any other. My father told me about him; how he had been the first man in space, his unassuming modesty, how he became a deputy of the Supreme Soviet, a hero for all the world, how he had died when his training jet crashed into trees. My father told me that it was a custom for all cosmonauts to visit Gagarin's office before a mission, to see the clock on the wall stopped at the moment of his death. Years later, I paid my own respects in the office.

The thing I remember most of all about my father, though, is holding me on his shoulders when I was five, taking me out into a cold winter evening to watch our Mir space station arc across the twilight sky. I reached out to grasp it and he held me higher, as if that might make a difference.

'Do you want to go up there sometime, Dimitri?'

'Do you have to be big?'

'No,' he said. 'But you have to be brave and strong. You'll do, one day.'

'And if I died would they stop the clock in my office as well?'

'You won't die,' my father said. Even though it was cold he had his shirt sleeves rolled up, his hair scratching against my skin.

'But if I did.'

'Of course they would. Just like Comrade Gagarin. And they'd make a hero of you as well.'

⮜⮞

The elevator doors open to a chill wind, howling in from the flat farmland beyond the city. The landing is open to the elements, only a low railing along one side. When I arrive at Nesha's apartment, half way along the building, the door is ajar. Nesha—for it can only be Nesha—is waiting in the gap, bony, long-nailed fingers curling around the edge of the door. I see half her face— her right eye, prematurely wrinkled skin, a wisp of grey hair. She looks much smaller, much older and frailer, than I ever dared to imagine.

'Whatever you have to show me, show me and go.'

'I'd really like to talk to you first.' I hold up my gloveless, numb-fingered hands. 'Everything I told you is true. I escaped from the psychiatric facility a few hours ago, and by now they'll be looking for me.'

'Then you should go now.'

'I was inside the Matryoshka, Nesha. Don't you want to hear what happened to me?'

She opens the door a tiny bit wider, showing me more of her face. She's old now but the younger Nesha hasn't been completely erased. I can still see the strong and determined women who stood by her beliefs, even when the state decided those beliefs were contrary to the official truth.

'I heard the rumours. They say you went insane.'

I give an easy shrug. 'I did, on the way home. It's the only thing that saved me. If I hadn't gone crazy, I wouldn't be standing here now.'

'You said there was something I had to know.'

'Give me a little of your time, then I'll be gone. That's my promise to you.'

Nesha looks back over her shoulder. She's wearing a knitted shawl of indeterminate colour. 'It isn't much warmer in here. When you called, I hoped you'd come to fix the central heating.' She pauses for a moment, mind working, then adds: 'I can give you something to drink, and maybe something better to wear. I still have some of my husband's old clothes—someone may as well get some use from them.'

'Thank you.'

'You shouldn't have come to see me. No good will come of it, for either us.'

'You might say the damage is already done.'

She lets me inside. Nesha might consider her apartment cold, but it's a furnace to me. After the wards and cubicles of the facility, it's bordering on the luxurious. There are a couple of items of old furniture, threadbare but otherwise serviceable. There's a low coffee table with faded plastic flowers in a vase. There are pictures on the walls, save for the part that's been painted over with television. It's beginning to flake off in the corners, so it won't be too long before someone comes along to redo it.

'I can't turn it off,' Nesha says, as if I've already judged her. 'You can scrape it away, but they just come and paint it on again. They take more care of that than they do the heating. And they don't like it if they think you'd done it deliberately, or tried to hide the television behind pictures.'

I remember the incessant televisions in the facility; the various strategies that the patients evolved to block them out or muffle the sound. 'I understand. You don't have to make allowances.'

'I don't like the world we live in. I'm old enough to remember when it was different.' Still standing up, she waves a hand dismissively, shooing away the memories of better times. 'Anyway, I don't hear so well these days. It's a blessing, I suppose.'

'Except it doesn't feel like one.' I point to one of the threadbare chairs. 'May I sit down?'

'Do what you like.'

I ease my aching bones into the chair. My damp clothes cling to me.

Nesha looks at me with something close to pity.

'Are you really the cosmonaut?'

'Yes.'

'I can make some tea.'

'Please. Anything hot.'

I watch her amble into the adjoining kitchen. Her clothes are still those of her early middle age, with allowance for infirmity and the cold. She wears old-looking jeans, several layers of jumpers, a scarf and the drab coloured shawl. Even though we're indoors she wears big fur boots. The clothes give her an illusion of bulk, but I can tell how thin she really is. Like a bird with a lot of puffed-up plumage, hiding delicate bones. There's also something darting, nervous and birdlike about the way she negotiates the claustrophobic angles of her apartment. I hear the clatter of a kettle, the squeak of a tap, a half-hearted dribble of water, then she returns.

'It'll take a while.'

'Everything does, these days. When I was younger, old people used to complain about the world getting faster and faster, leaving them behind. That isn't how it seems to you and I. We've left the world behind—we've kept up, but it hasn't.'

'How old are you?' she asks.

'Fifty one.'

'Not what I'd call old. I have nearly twenty years on you.' But her eyes measure me and I know what she's thinking. I look older, beyond any doubt. The mission took its toll on me, but so did the facility. There were times when I looked in the mirror with a jolt of non-recognition, a stranger's face staring back at me. 'Something bad happened to you out there, didn't it,' she said.

'To all of us.'

She makes the tea. 'You think I envy you,' she says, as I sip from my cup.

'Why would you envy me?'

'Because you went out there, because you saw it up close, because you went inside it. You cosmonauts think all astronomers are the same. You go out into space and look at the universe through a layer of armoured glass, if you're lucky. Frosted with your own breath, blurring everything on the other side. Like visiting someone in a prison, not being able to touch them. You think we envy you that.'

'Some might say it's better to get that close, than not go at all.'

'I stayed at home. I touched the universe with my mind, through mathematics. No glass between us then—just a sea of numbers.' Nesha looks at me sternly. 'Numbers are truth. It doesn't get any more intimate than numbers.'

'It's enough that we both reached out, wouldn't you say?' I offer her a conciliatory smile—I haven't come to pick a fight about the best way to apprehend nature. 'The fact is, no one's doing much of that any more. There's no money for science and there's certainly none for space travel. But we did something great. They can write us out of history, but it doesn't change what we did.'

'And me?'

'You were part of it. I'd read all your articles, long before I was selected for the mission. That's why I came to see you, all that time ago. But long before that—I knew what I wanted to do with my life. I was a young man when the Matryoshka arrived, but not so young that I didn't have dreams and plans.'

'You must be sorry about that now.'

'Sometimes. Not always. No more than you regret what you did.'

'It was different back then, between the Soviets. If you believed something, you said it.'

'So you don't regret a word of it.'

'I had it easier than he did.'

Silence. I look at a photograph on the coffee table—a young woman and a young man, holding hands in front of some grand old church or cathedral I don't recognise, in some European city I'll never see. They have bright clothes with slogans on, sunglasses, ski hats, and they're both smiling. The sky is a hard primary blue, as if it's been daubed in poster paint. 'That's him,' I say.

'Gennadi was a good man. But he never knew when to shut his mouth. That was his problem. The new men wanted to take us back to the old ways. Lots of people thought that was a good idea, too. The problem was, not all of us did. I was born in nineteen seventy five. I'm old enough to remember what it was like before Gorbachev. It wasn't all that wonderful, believe me.'

'Tell me about Gennadi. How did he get involved?'

'Gennadi was a scientist to begin with—an astronomer like me, in the same institute. That's how we met. But his heart was elsewhere. Politics took up more and more of his time.'

'He was a politician?'

'An activist. A journalist and a blogger. Do you remember the internet, Dimitri?'

'Just barely.' It's something from my childhood, like foreign tourists and contrails in the sky.

'It was a tool the authorities couldn't control. That made them nervous. They couldn't censor it, or take it down—not then. But they could take down the people behind it, like Gennadi. So that's what they did.'

'I'm sorry.'

'It's all in the past now. We had our time together; that's all that matters. Perhaps if I hadn't made such a noise about my findings, perhaps if I hadn't angered the wrong people... 'Nesha stops speaking. All of a sudden I feel shamefully intrusive. What right have I have to barge in on this old woman, to force her to think about the way things used to be? But I can't leave, not having come this far. 'His clothes,' she says absent-mindedly. 'I don't know why I kept them all this time, but perhaps you can use them.'

I put down the tea. 'Are you certain?'

'It's what Gennadi would have wanted. Always very practically-minded, Gennadi. Go into the room behind you, the cupboard on the left. Take what you can use.'

'Thank you.'

Even though I'm beginning to warm up, it's good to change out of the sodden old clothes. Gennadi must have been shorter than me, his trousers not quite reaching my ankles, but I'm in no mood to complain. I find a vest, a shirt and an old grey sweater that's been repaired a number of times. I find lace-up shoes that I can wear with two layers of socks. I wash my hands and face in the bedroom basin, straightening back my hair, but there's nothing I can do to tidy or trim my beard. I had plans to change my appearance so far as I was able, but all of a sudden I know how futile that'd be. They'll find me again, even if it takes a little longer. They'd only have to take one look in my eyes to know who I am.

'Do they fit?' Nesha asks, when I return to the main room.

'Like a glove. You've been very kind. I can't ever repay this.'

'Start by telling me why you're here. Then—although I can't say I'm sorry for a little company—you can be on your way, before you get both of us into trouble.'

I return to the same seat I used before. It's snowing again, softly. In the distance the dark threads of railway lines stretch between two anonymous buildings. I remember what the snowplough driver said. In this weather, I can forget about buses. No one's getting in or out of Zvezdniy Gorodok unless they have party clearance and a waiting Zil.

'I came to tell you that you were right,' I say. 'After all these years.'

'About the Matryoshka?'

'Yes.'

'I've known I was right for nearly thirty years. I didn't need you to come and tell me.'

'Doesn't it help to know that someone else believes you now?'

'Truth is truth, no matter who else believes it.'

'You constructed a hypothesis to fit the data,' I said. 'It was a sound hypothesis, in that it was testable. But that's all it ever was. You never got to see it tested.'

She regards me with steely-eyed intensity, the earlier Nesha Petrova burning through the mask of the older one. 'I did. The second apparition.'

'Where they proved you wrong?'

'So they said.'

'They were wrong. I know. But they used it to crush you, to mock you, to bury you. But we went inside. We penetrated Shell 3. After that—everything was different.'

'Does it matter now?'

'I think it does.' Now is the moment. The thing I've come all this way to give Nesha, the thing that's been in my pyjama pocket, now in the trousers. I take it out, the prize folded in a white handkerchief.

I pass the bundle across the coffee table. 'This is for you.'

Nesha takes it warily. She unwraps the handker- chief and blinks at the little metal box it had contained. She picks it up gently, holds it before her eyes and pinches her fingers around the little handle that sticks out from one side.

'Turn it.'

'What?'

'Turn the handle.'

She does as I say, gently and hesitantly at first, as if fearful that the handle will snap off in her fingers.

The box emits a series of tinkling notes. Because Nesha is turning the handle so slowly, it's hard to make out the melody.

'I don't understand. You came all this way to give me this?'

'I did.'

'Then the rumours were right,' Nesha says. 'You did go mad after all.'

⊖⊖

Falling inward, the Progress began to pass through another swarm of free-flying obstacles. Like those of Shell 1, the components of Shell 2 were all but invisible to the naked eye—dark as space itself, and only a fraction of a kelvin warmer than the cosmic microwave background. The wireframe display started showing signs of fuzziness, as if the computer was having trouble decoding the radar returns. The objects were larger and had a different shape to the ones in the outer shell— these were more like rounded pebbles or all-enveloping turtle-shells, wide as cities. They were covered in scales or plaques which moved around in a weird, oozing fashion, like jostling continents on a planet with vigorous plate tectonics. Similarly lethal field lines bound them, but this far in the predictive model became a lot less trustworthy.

No runaway Chinese probe had ever collided with Shell 2, so we had no good idea how brittle the objects were. A second apparition probe operated by the

European Space Agency had tried to land and sample one of the Shell 2 obstacles, but without success. That wouldn't stop Galenka from making her own attempt.

She picked a target, wove around the field lines and came in close enough to fire the sticky anchors onto one of the oozing platelets. The Progress wound itself in on electric winches until it was close enough to extend its tools and manipulators.

'Damn camera's sticking again. And I keep losing antenna lock.'

'It's what they pay you for,' I said.

'Trying to be helpful, Dimitri?'

'Doing my best.'

She had her hands in the waldos again. Her eyes darted from screen to screen. Never having trained for Progress operations, I couldn't make much sense of the displays myself. It looked as if she was playing six or seven weirdly abstract computer games at the same time, manipulating symbols according to arcane and ever-shifting rules. I could only hope that she was holding her ground.

'Cutting head can't get traction. Whatever that stuff is, it's harder than diamond. Nothing for the claws to grip, either. I'm going to try the laser.'

I tensed as she swung the laser into play. How would the Matryoshka respond to our burning a hole in it? With the same cosmic indifference that it had shown when the Chinese robot had rammed it, or when the American probe intersected its field lines? Nothing in our experience offered guidance. Perhaps it had tolerated us until now, and would interpret the laser as the first genuinely hostile action. In which case losing the Progress might be the least of our worries.

'Picking up ablation products,' Galenka said, eyeing the trembling registers of a gas chromatograph readout. 'Laser's cutting into *something*, whatever it is. Lots of carbon. Some noble gases and metals: iron, vanadium, some other stuff I'm not too sure about right now. Let's see if I can cut away a sample.'

The laser etched a circle into the surface of the platelet. With the beam kept at an angle to the surface, it was eventually possible to isolate a cone-shaped piece of the material. Galenka used an epoxy-tipped sucker to extract the fist-sized sample, which already seemed to be in the proces of fusing back into the main structure.

'Well done.'

She grinned at me. 'Let's take a few more while our luck's holding, shall we?'

She pulled out of the waldo controls, disengaged the sticky anchors and applied translational thrust, shifting the Progress to a different platelet.

'You sure you don't want to take a break? We can hold here for hours if we have to, especially with the anchors.'

'I'm fine, Dimitri.' But I noticed that Galenka's knuckles were tight on the joystick, the effort of piloting beginning to show. There was a chisel-sharp crease in the skin on the side of her mouth that only came when she was concentrating. 'Fine but a little hungry, if you must know. You want to do something useful, you can fetch me some food.'

'I think that might be within my capabilities,' I said.

I pushed away from the piloting position, expertly inserting myself onto a weightless trajectory that sent me careening through one of the narrow connecting throats that led from one of the *Tereshkova*'s modules to the next.

By any standards she was a large spacecraft. Nuclear power had brought us to the Matryoshka. The *Tereshkova*'s main engine was a "variable specific impulse magnetic rocket": a VASIMIR drive. It was an old design that had been dusted down and made to work when the requirements of our mission became clear. The point of the VASIMIR (it was an American acronym, but it *sounded* appropriately Russian) was that it could function in a dual mode, giving not us only the kick to escape Earth orbit, but also months of low-impulse cruise thrust, to take us all the way to the artefact and back. It would get us all the way home again, too— whereupon we'd climb into our Soyuz re-entry vehicle and detach from the mothership. The Progress would come down on autopilot, laden with alien riches—that was the plan, anyway.

Like all spacecraft, the *Tereshkova* looked like a ransacked junk shop inside. Any area of the ship that wasn't already in use as a screen or control panel or equipment hatch or analysis laboratory or food dispenser or life-support system was something to hold onto, or kick off from, or rest against, or tie things onto. Technical manuals floated in mid-air, tethered to the wall. Bits of computer drifted around the ship on pilgrimages of their own, until one of us needed some cable or connector. Photos of our family, drawings made by our children, were tacked to the walls between panels and grab rails. The whole thing stank like an armpit and made so much noise that most of us kept earplugs in when we didn't need to talk.

But it was home, of a sort. A stinking, noisy shithole of a home, but still the best we had.

I hadn't seen Yakov as I moved through the ship, but that wasn't any cause for alarm. As the specialist in charge of the *Tereshkova*'s flight systems, his duty load had eased now that we had arrived on station at the artefact. He had been busy during the cruise phase, so we couldn't begrudge him a little time off, especially as he was going to have to nurse the ship home again. So, while Baikonur gave him a certain number of housekeeping tasks to attend to, Yakov had more time to himself than Galenka or I. If he wasn't in his quarters, there were a dozen other places on the ship where he could find some privacy, if not peace and quiet. We all had our favorite spots, and we were careful not to intrude on each other when we needed some personal time.

So I had no reason to sense anything unusual as I selected and warmed a meal for Galenka. But as the microwave chimed readiness, a much louder alarm began shrieking throughout the ship. Red emergency lights started flashing. The general distress warning meant that the ship had detected something anomalous. Without further clarification, it could be almost anything: a fault with the VASIMIR, a hull puncture, a life-support system failure, a hundred other problems. All that the alarm told me was that the ship deemed the problem critical, demanding immediate attention.

I grabbed a handrail and propelled myself to the nearest monitor. Text was already scrolling on it.

*Unscheduled activity in hatch three,* said the words.

I froze for a few moments, not so much in panic as out of a need to pause and concentrate, to assess the situation and decide on the best course of action. But I didn't need much time to reflect. Since Galenka was still at her station, still guiding the Progress, it was obvious what the problem was. Yakov was trying to escape from the *Tereshkova.*

As if we were still in Star City.

There was no automatic safety mechanism to prevent that door from being opened. It was assumed that if anyone did try and open it, they must have a valid reason for doing so—venting air into space, for instance, to quench a fire.

I pushed myself through the module, through the connecting throat, through the next module. The alarm was drilling into my head. If Yakov really did think that the ship was still in Russia, he wouldn't be concerned about decompression. He wouldn't be concerned about whether or not he was wearing a suit.

He just wanted to get out.

I reached a red locker marked with a lightning flash and threw back the heavy duty latches. I expected to see three tasers, bound with security foils.

There were no tasers—just the remains of the foil and the recessed foam shapes where the stunners had fitted.

'Fuck,' I said, realising that Yakov was ahead of me; that he had opened the locker—against all rules; it was only supposed to be touched in an emergency—and taken the weapons.

I pushed through another connecting throat, scraping my hand against sharp metal until it bled, then corkscrewed through ninety degrees to reach the secondary throat that led to the number three hatch.

I could already see Yakov at the end of it. Braced against the wall, he was turning the yellow cartwheel that undid the door's locking mechanism. When he was done, it would only take a twist of the handle to free the hatch. The air pressure behind it would slam it open in an instant, and both of us would be sucked into space long before emergency bulkhead seals protected the rest of the ship. I tried to work out which way we were facing now. Would it be a long fall back to the Sun, or an inglorious short-cut to the Matryoshka?

'Yakov, please,' I called. 'Don't open the door.'

He kept working the wheel, but looked back at me over his shoulder. 'No good, Dimitri. I've figured this out even if you haven't. None of this is real. We're not really out here, parked next to the Matryoshka. We're just rehearsing for it, running through another simulation.'

I tried to ride with his logic. 'Then let's see the simulation through to the end.'

'Don't you get it? This is all a test. They want to see how alert we are. They want to see that we're still capable of picking up on the details that don't fit.'

The blood was spooling out of my hand, forming a chain of scarlet droplets. I pushed the wound to my mouth and sucked at it. 'Like weightlessness? How would they ever fake that, Dimitri?'

He let go of the wheel with one hand and touched the back of his neck. 'The implants. They fool with your inner ear, make you think you're floating.'

'That's your GLONASS transponder. It's so they can track and recover our bodies if the re-entry goes wrong.'

'That's what they told us.' He kept on turning the wheel.

'You open that door, you're a dead man. You'll kill me and probably Galenka as well.'

'Listen to me,' he said with fierce insistence. 'This is not real. We're in Star City, my friend. We're still back in Russia. The whole point of this exercise is to measure our alertness, our ability to see through delusional constructs. Escaping from the ship is the objective, the end-state.'

Reasoned argument clearly wasn't going to get me anywhere. I gave myself a hard shove in his direction, hoping to overwhelm him with sheer momentum. But Yakov was faster. His hand sprung to his pocket and came out holding one of the tasers, aimed straight at me. The barbs sprang out and contacted my chest. Never having been shot before I wasn't remotely ready for the pain. It seemed to crush me into a little ball of concentrated fire, like an insect curling under the heat from a magnifying glass. I let out a brief yelp, biting my tongue, and then I didn't even have the energy to scream. The barbs were still in me. Bent double, blood dribbling from my hand and mouth, I lost all contact with the ship. Drifting, I saw Yakov leave the taser floating in mid-air while he returned his attention to the wheel and redoubled his efforts.

'You stupid fucker,' I heard Galenka say, behind me.

I didn't know whether she meant Yakov—for trying to escape—or me, for trying to stop him on my own. Maybe she meant both of us.

The pain of the discharge was beginning to ebb. I could just begin to think about speaking again.

'Got a taser,' I heard myself say, as if from a distance.

'Good. So have I.' I felt Galenka push past me, something hard in her hand. Then I heard the strobing crackle of another taser. I kept drifting around, until the door came into view again. Through blurred and slitted eyes, I saw Yakov twitching against the metal. Galenka had fired barbs into him; now she was holding the prongs of the taser against his abdomen, the blue worm of a spark writhing between.

I reached out a hand and managed to steady myself. The pain had now all but gone, but I was enveloped in nausea and a tingling all-body version of pins and needles.

'You can stop now.'

She gave the taser one last prod, then withdrew it. Yakov remained still, slumped and unconscious against the door.

'I say we kill the fucker now.'

I wiped the blood from my lips. 'I know how you feel. But we need him to get us home. If there's the slightest problem with the engine…'

'Anything happens, mission control can help us.'

I worked my way down to the door. 'He's not going to do this again. We can sedate him, wrap him in duct-tape and confine him to one of the modules if necessary. Until Baikonur advise.'

Galenka pushed her own taser back into her pocket, with the barbs dangling loose on their springy wires. She started turning the wheel in the opposite direction, grunting at first with the effort.

'This was a close call.'

'You were right—I should have been more worried about him than I was. I didn't think he was really serious about all that Star City stuff. I mean, not *this* serious.'

'He's a basket case, Dimitri. That means there are only two sane people left on this ship, and I'm being generous.'

'Do you think Baikonur will be able to help?'

'They'd better. Anything goes wrong on this ship, we need him to fix it. And he's not going to be much use to us doped to his eyeballs.'

We manhandled the stunned Yakov back into the main part of the *Tereshkova*. Already I could tell that he was only lightly unconscious, and that we'd have a struggle on our hands if he came around now. He was mumbling under his breath. Sweat began to bead on my forehead. Why the fuck did this have to happen to us?

'What do you reckon we should do? Confine him to his quarters?'

'And have him loose aboard the ship again, looking for a way to escape?'

'I'm not sure we have any other choice.'

'We lock him in the forward module,' Galenka said decisively. 'He'll be safe in there. We can seal the connecting lock from our side, until Baikonur come up with a treatment regime. In the meantime we dose him on sedatives, put him under for as long as we can. I don't want that lunatic running around when I'm trying to steer the Progress through Shell 3.'

I breathed in hard, trying to focus. 'Where is it now?'

'Still anchored to one of the Shell 2 platelets. I'd like to take a few more samples before I detach, but from then on it's seat of the pants stuff.'

She was right: it was a good plan. Better than anything I could come up with, at any rate. We took him forward to the orbiter, opened a medical kit and injected him with the sedative. I took out a tube of disinfectant and a roll of bandage for my gashed hand. Yakov stopped mumbling and became more pliant, like a big rag doll. We duct-taped him into a sleeping hammock and locked the door on him.

'He was pissing me off anyway,' Galenka said.

⊕⊖

I move back from the window in Nesha's apartment. Zvezdniy Gorodok is stirring to hypothermic half-life. The snow's still coming down, though in fitful flurries rather than a steady fall. When a Zil pulls onto the street I feel a tightness in my throat. But the limousine stops, releasing its passenger, and moves on. The man strolls across the concrete concourse into one of the adjoining buildings, a briefcase swinging from his hand. He might have anything in that briefcase—a gun, a syringe, a lie detector. But he has no business here.

'You think they're looking for you.'

'I know it.'

'Then where are you going to go?'

Out into the cold and the snow to die, I think. But I smile and say nothing.

'Is it really so bad in the facility? Do they really treat you so badly?'

I return to my seat. Nesha's poured me another cup of tea, which—her views on my sanity notwithstanding—I take as an invitation to remain. 'Most of them don't treat me badly at all—they're not monsters or sadists. I'm too precious to them for that. They don't beat me, or electrocute me, and the drugs they give me, the things they do to me, they're not to make me docile or to punish me. Doctor Kizim, he's even kind to me. He spends a lot of time talking to me, trying to get me to remember details I might have forgotten. It's pointless, though. I've already remembered all that I'm ever going to. My brain feels like a pan that's been scrubbed clean.'

'Did Doctor Kizim help you to escape?'

'I've asked myself the same question. Did he mean for me to steal his coat? Did he sense that I was intending to leave? He must have known I wouldn't get far without it.'

'What about the others? Were you allowed to see them?'

I shake my head. 'They kept us apart the whole time Yakov and Galenka were still alive. We were questioned and examined separately. Even though we'd spent all those months in the ship, they didn't want us contaminating each other's accounts.'

'So you never really got to know what happened to the others.'

'I know that they both died. Galenka went first—she took the highest dosage when the VASIMIR's shielding broke down. Yakov was a little luckier, but not much. I never got to see either of them while they were still alive.'

'Why didn't you get a similar dosage?'

'Yakov was mad to begin with. Then he got better, or at least decided he was better off working with us than against us. We let him out of the module where we were keeping him locked up. That was after Galenka and I got back from the Matryoshka.'

'And then?'

'It was my turn to go a little mad. Inside the machine—something touched us. It got into our heads. It affected me more than it did Galenka. On the return trip, they had no choice but to confine me to the forward module.'

'The thing that saved you.'

'I was further from the engine when it went wrong. Inverse square laws. My dosage was negligible.'

'You accept that they died, despite having no evidence.'

'I believe what Doctor Kizim told me. I trusted him. He had no reason to lie. He was already putting his career at risk by giving me this information. Maybe more than his career. A good man.'

'Did he know the other two?'

'No; he only ever treated me. That was part of the methodology. Strange things had happened during the early months of the debriefing. The doctors and surgeons got too close to us, too involved. After we came back from the Matryoshka, there was something different about us. It affected us all, even Yakov, who hadn't gone inside. Just being close to it was enough.'

'Different in what way?' Nesha asks.

'It began in small ways, while we were still on the *Tereshkova*. Weird slips. Mistakes that didn't make sense. As if our identities, our personalities and memories, were blurring. On the way home, I sit at the computer keyboard and find myself typing Yakov's name and password into the system, as if he's sitting inside me. A few days later Galenka wakes up and tells me she dreamed she was in Klushino, a place she's never visited.' I pause, trying to find words that would not make me sound crazy. 'It was as if something in the machine had touched us and removed some fundamental barrier in our heads, some wall or moat that keeps one person from becoming another. When the silver fluid got into us …'

'I don't understand. How could the doctors get too close to you? What happened to them?'

I sense her uneasiness; the realisation that she may well be sharing her room with a lunatic. I have never pretended to be entirely sane, but it must only be now that the white bones of true madness are beginning to show through my skin.

'I didn't mean to alarm you, Nesha. I'll be gone shortly, I promise you. Why don't you tell me what it was like for you, back when it all began?'

'You know my story.'

'I'd still like to hear it from you. From the day it arrived. How it changed you.'

'You were old enough to remember it. You already told me that.'

'But I wasn't an astronomer, Nesha. I was just a twenty year old kid with some ideas about being a cosmonaut. You were how old, exactly?'

'Forty years. I'd been a professional astronomer for fifteen or sixteen of them, by then.' She becomes reflective, as if it's only now that she has given that time of her life any thought. 'I'd been lucky, really. I'd made professor, which meant I didn't have to grub around for funding every two years. I had to do my share of lecturing, and fighting my corner for the department, but I still had plenty of time for independent research. I was still in love with science, too. My little research area—stellar pulsation modes—it wasn't the most glamorous.' She gives a rueful smile. 'They didn't fight to put our faces on the covers of magazine, or give us lucrative publishing deals to talk about how we were uncovering the mysteries of the universe, touching the face of God. But we knew it was solid science, important to the field as a whole.' She leans forward to make a point. 'Astronomy's like a cathedral, Dimitri. The ones putting the gold on the top spire get all the glory, but they'd be nothing without a solid foundation. That's where we were—down in the basement, down in the crypt, making sure it was all anchored to firm ground. Fundamental stellar physics. Not very exotic compared to mapping the large scale universe, or probing the event horizons of black holes. But vital all the same.'

'I don't doubt it.'

'I can remember that afternoon when the news came in. Gennadi and I were in my office. It was a bright day, with the blinds drawn. It was the end of the week and we were looking forward to a few days off. We had tickets to see a band in town that night. We just had one thing we wanted to get sorted before we finished. A paper we'd been working on had come back from the referee with a load of snotty comments, and we didn't quite agree on how to deal with them. I wanted to write back to the journal and request a different referee. The referee on our paper was anonymous, but I was sure I knew who it was—a slimy, womanising prick who'd made a pass at me at a conference in Trieste, and wasn't going to let me forget that I'd told him where to get off.'

I smile. 'You must have been fierce in your day.'

'Well, maybe it wasn't him—but we still needed a different referee. Gennadi, meanwhile, thought we should sit back and do what the referee was telling us. Which meant running our models again, which meant a week of time on the department supercomputer. Normally, that would have meant going right back to the start of the queue. But there was a gap in the schedule— another group had just pulled out of their slot, because they couldn't get their software to compile properly. We could have their slot—but only if we got our model up and running that evening, with all the modifications the referee wanted us to make.'

'You weren't going to make it to that band.'

'That was when the IAU telegram came in to my inbox. I didn't even open it at first; it wasn't as if IAU telegrams were exactly unusual. It probably just meant that a supernova had gone off in a remote galaxy, or that some binary star was undergoing a nova. Nothing I needed to get excited about.'

'But that wasn't what it was about.'

'It was the Matryoshka, of course—the emergence event, when it came into our solar system. A sudden influx of cosmic rays, triggering half the monitoring telescopes and satellites in existence. They all turned to look at the point where the machine had come in. A flash of energy that intense, it could only be a gamma-ray burst, happening in some distant galaxy. That's what everyone thought it was, especially as the Matryoshka came in high above the ecliptic, and well out of the plane of the galaxy. It looked extragalactic, not some local event. Sooner or later, though, they crunched the numbers—triangulated from the slightly different pointing angles of the various spacecraft and telescopes, the slightly different detection times of the event— and they realised that, whatever this was, it had happened within one light hour of the Sun. Not so much on our doorstep, cosmically speaking, as in our house, making itself at home.' The memory seems to please her. 'There was some wild theorizing to begin with. Everything from a piece of antimatter colliding with a comet, a quantum black hole evaporating, to the illegal test of a Chinese super-weapon in deep space. Of course, it was none of those things. It was spacetime opening wide enough to vomit out a machine the size of Tasmania.'

'It was a while before they found the Matryoshka itself.'

Nesha nods. 'You try finding something that dark, when you don't even know in which direction it's moving.'

'Even from the *Tereshkova*, it was hard to believe it was actually out there.'

'To begin with, we still didn't know what to make of it. The layered structure confused the hell out of us. We weren't used to analysing anything like that. It was artificial, clearly, but it wasn't made of solid parts. It was like a machine caught in the instant of blowing up, but which was still working, still doing whatever it was sent to do. Without getting closer, we could only resolve the structure in the outer layer. We didn't start calling it Shell 1 until we knew there were deeper strata. The name Matryoshka didn't come until after the first fly-by probes, when we glimpsed Shell 2. The Americans called it the Easter Egg for a little while, but eventually everyone started using the Russian name.'

I know that when she talks about "we", she means the astronomical community as a whole, rather than her own efforts. Nesha's involvement—the involvement that had first made her famous, then ruined her reputation, then her life—did not come until later.

The emergence event—the first apparition—caught humanity entirely unawares. The Matryoshka had come out of its wormhole mouth—if that was what it was—on an elliptical, sun-circling trajectory similar to a periodic comet. The only thing non-cometary was the very steep inclination to the ecliptic. It made reaching the Matryoshka problematic, except when it was swinging near the Sun once every twelve years. Even with a massive international effort, there was no way to send dedicated probes out to meet the artefact and match its velocity. The best anyone could do was fling smart pebbles at it, hoping to learn as much as possible in the short window while they slammed past. Probes that had been intended for Mars or Venus were hastily repurposed for the Matryoshka flyby, where time and physics made that possible. It was more like the mad scramble of some desperate, last-ditch war effort than anything seen in peacetime.

There were, of course, dissenting voices. Some people thought the prudent thing would be to wait and see what the Matryoshka had in mind for us. By and large, they were ignored. The thing had arrived here, hadn't it? The least it could expect was a welcome party.

As it was, the machine appeared completely oblivious to the attention—as it had continued to do through the second apparition. The third apparition—that was different, of course. But then again our provocation had been of an entirely different nature.

After the probes had gone by, there was data to analyse. Years of it. The Matryoshka had fallen out of reach of our instruments and robots, but we had more than enough to keep busy until the next apparition. Plans were already being drawn up for missions to rendezvous with the object and penetrate that outer layer. Robots next time, but who knew what might be possible in the twenty four years between the first and third apparitions?

'The scientists who'd had their missions redirected wanted a first look at the Matryoshka data,' Nesha says. 'The thinking was that they'd get exclusive access to it for six months.'

'You can't blame them for that.'

'There was still an outcry. It was felt that an event of this magnitude demanded the immediate release of all the data to the community. To the whole world, in fact. Anyone who wanted it was welcome to it. Of course, unless they had a lightning fast internet connection, about ten million terabytes of memory, expertise in hypercube number-crunching, their own Cray … they couldn't even begin to scratch the surface. There were collaborative efforts, millions of people downloading a fragment of the data and analysing it using spare CPU cycles, but they still couldn't beat the resources of a single well-equipped academic department with a tame supercomputer in the basement. Above all else, we had all the analysis tools at hand, and we knew how to use them. But it was still a massive cake to eat in one bite.'

'And did you?'

'No—it made much more sense to focus on what we were good at. The data hinted that the elements of the outer layer—Shell 1—were bound together by some kind of force-field. The whole thing was breathing in and out, the components moving as if tied together by a complex web of elastic filaments.' She shapes her fingers around an invisible ball and makes the ball swell and contract. 'The thing is, stars breathe as well. The pulsation modes in a solar-type star aren't the same as the pulsation modes in the Matryoshka. But we could still use the same methods, the same tools and tricks, to get a handle on them. And of course, there was a point to all of that. Map the pulsations in a star and you can probe the deep interior, in exactly the same way that earthquakes tell us about the structure of the Earth. There was every expectation that the Matryoshka's pulsations might tell us something about the inside of that as well.'

'I guess you didn't have a clue what you'd actually find.'

Nesha gives a brief, derisive laugh. 'Of course not. I wasn't thinking in those terms at all. I was just thinking of frequencies, harmonics, Fourier analysis, caustic surfaces. I wasn't thinking of fucking *music*.'

'Tell me how it felt.'

'The first time I ran the analysis, and realised that the pulsations could be broken down into notes on the western chromatic scale? Like I was the victim of a bad practical joke, someone in the department messing with the data.'

'And when you realised you weren't being hoaxed?'

'I still didn't *believe* it—not to begin with. I thought I must have screwed up in my analysis somewhere, introduced harmonics that weren't real. I stripped the tools down and put them together again. Same story— notes, chords, melody and counterpoint. Music. That's when I started accepting the reality of it. Whatever we were dealing with—whatever had come to find us— wasn't what we had assumed. This wasn't just some dumb invention, some alien equivalent of the probes we had been sending out. The Matryoshka was a different order of machine. Something clever and complex enough to sing to itself. Or, just possibly, to us.' Nesha hesitates and looks at me with an unwavering gaze. 'And it was singing our music. Russian music.'

'I know,' I say. 'It's been in my head since I came back.'

⋐⋑

No one had been this deep before.

The Progress had travelled fifty kilometres into the Matryoshka—through two layers of orbiting obstruction, each of which was ten kilometres in depth, and through two open volumes fifteen kilometres thick. Beneath lay the most difficult part of its journey so far. Though the existence of Shell 3 had been known since the second apparition, no hard data existed on conditions beneath it.

The barrier was actually a pair of tightly nested spheres, one slightly smaller than the other. The shell's material was as dark as anything already encountered, but—fortuitously for us—the spheres had holes in them, several dozen circular perforations ranging in width from one to three kilometres, spotted around the spheres in what appeared to be an entirely random arrangement. The pattern of holes was the same in both spheres, but because they were rotating at different speeds, on different, slowly precessing axes, the holes only lined up occasionally. During those windows, glimpses opened up into the heart of the Matryoshka. A blue-green glow shone through the winking gaps in Shell 3, hinting at luminous depths.

Shortly we'd know.

'How's he doing?' Galenka asked, from the pilot's position. I had just returned from the orbiter, where I had been checking on Yakov. I had fixed a medical cuff to his wrist, so that Baikonur could analyse his blood chemistry.

'Not much change since last time. He just looks at me. Doesn't say or do anything.'

'We should up the medication.' She tapped keys, adjusting one of the Progress's camera angles. She was holding station, hovering a few kilometres over Shell 3. Talking out of the side of her mouth she said: 'Put him into a coma until we really need him.'

'I talked to Baikonur. They recommend holding him at the current dosage until they've run some tests.'

'Easy for them to say, half the solar system away.'

'They're the experts, not us.'

'If you say so.'

'I think we should let them handle this one. It's not like we don't have other things to occupy our minds, is it?'

'You have a point there, comrade.'

'Are you happy about taking her in? You've been in the chair for a long time now.'

'It's what we came to do. Progress systems are dropping like flies, anyway—I give this ship about six hours before it dies on us. I think it's now or never.'

I could only bow to her superior wisdom in this matter.

In the years since the last apparition, the complex motion of the spheres had been subjected to enormous scrutiny. It had been a triumph to map the holes in the interior sphere. Despite this, no watertight algorithm had ever been devised to predict the window events with any precision. The spheres slowed down and sped up unpredictably, making a nonsense of long-range forecasts. Unless a window was in view, the movement of the inner sphere could not be measured. Radar bounced off its flawless surface as if the thing was motionless.

All Galenka could do was wait until a window event began, then make a run for it—hoping that the aperture remained open long enough for the Progress to pass through. Analysis of all available data showed that window events occurred, on average, once in every seventy two minute interval. But that was just an average. Two window events could fall within minutes of each other, or there might be a ten hour wait before the next one. Timing was tight—the Progress would have to begin its run within seconds of the window opening, if it had a chance of slipping through. I didn't envy Galenka sitting there with her finger on the trigger, like a gunslinger waiting for her opponent to twitch.

In the event, a useful window—one that she could reach, in the allowed time—opened within forty minutes of our conversation. Looking over her shoulder at the screens, I could scarcely detect any change in Shell 3. Only when the Progress was already committed—moving too quickly to stop or change course—did a glimmer of blue-green light reassure me that the window was indeed opening. Even then, it hardly seemed possible that the Progress would have time to pass through the winking eye.

Of course, that was exactly what happened. Only a slight easing of the crease on the side of Galenka's mouth indicated that she was, for now, breathing easier. We both knew that this triumph might be exceedingly short-lived, since the Progress would now find it even more difficult to remain in contact with the *Tereshkova*. Since no man-made signal could penetrate Shell 3, comms could only squirt through when a window was open, in whatever direction that happened to be. The swarm of relay microsats placed around the Matryoshka were intended to intercept these burst transmissions and relay them back to the *Tereshkova*. Its puppet-strings all but severed, the robotic spacecraft would be relying more and more on the autonomous decision-making of its onboard computers.

I knew that the mission planners had subjected the Progress to every eventuality, every scenario, they could dream up. I also knew that none of those planners seriously expected the secrets of the Matryoshka to bear the slightest resemblance to their imaginings. If it did, they'd be brutally disappointed.

The rear-looking camera showed the window sealing behind the Progress. The inside surface of Shell 3 was as pitilessly dark as its outer skin, yet all else was aglow. I shivered with an almost religious ecstasy. Soon the secrets revealed here would be in the hands of the entire human species, but for now—for a delicious and precious interval—the only two souls granted this privilege were Galenka and I. No other thinking creature had seen this far.

Beneath Shell 3 was another empty volume—Gap 3. Then there was another sphere. We were looking at the central sixty kilometres of the Matryoshka, three quarters of the way to whatever lay at its heart. Shell 4 looked nothing like the dark machinery we had already passed through. This was more like a prickly fruit, a nastily evolved bacterium or some fantastically complex coral formation. The surface of the sphere was barely visible, lost under a spiky, spiny accretion of spokes and barbs and twisted unicorn horns, pushing out into the otherwise empty band gap for many kilometres. Lacy webs of matter bridged one spike to the next. Muscular structures, like the roots of enormous trees, entwined the bases of the largest outgrowths. It was all ablaze with blue-green light, like a glass sculpture lit from within. The light wavered and pulsed. Shell 3 did not look like something which had been designed and built, but rather something which had grown, wildly and unpredictably. It was wonderful and terrifying.

Then the signal ended. The Progress was on its own now, relying on its hardwired wits.

'You did well,' I told Galenka.

She said nothing. She was already asleep. Her head did not loll in zero gravity, her jaw did not droop open, but her eyes were closed and her hand had slackened on the joystick. Only then did I realise how utterly exhausted she must have been. But I imagined her dreams were peaceful ones. She had not failed the mission. She had not failed Mother Russia and the Second Soviet.

I left her sleeping, then spent two hours attending to various housekeeping tasks aboard the *Tereshkova*. Since we were only able to use the low-gain antenna—the high-gain antenna had failed shortly after departure— the data that the Progress had already sent back needed to be organised and compressed before it could be sent onwards to Earth. All the data stored aboard the *Tereshkova* would get home eventually—assuming, of course, that we did—but in the meantime I was anxious to provide Baikonur with what I regarded as the highlights. All the while I checked for updates from the Progress, but no signal had yet been detected.

Without waiting for mission control to acknowledge the data package, I warmed some food for myself, took a nip of vodka from my private supply, and then carried my meal into the part of the *Tereshkova* loosely designated as the commons/recreational area. It was the brightest part of the ship, with plastic flowers and ornaments, tinsel, photographs, postcards and children's paintings stuck to the walls. I stationed myself against a wall and watched television, flicking through the various uplink feeds while spooning food into my mouth. I skipped soaps, quizzes and chat shows until I hit the main state news channel. The *Tereshkova* had been big news during its departure, but had fallen from the headlines during the long and tedious cruise to the Matryoshka. Now we were again a top-listed item once more, squeezing out stories of indomitable Soviet enterprise and laughable Capitalist failure.

The channel informed its viewers that the ship had successfully launched a robotic probe through Shells 1 and 2, a triumph equal to anything achieved during the last two apparitions, and one which—it was confidently expected—would soon be surpassed. The data already returned to Earth, the channel said, offered a bounty that would keep the keenest minds engaged for many years. Nor would this data be hoarded by Russia alone, for with characteristic Soviet generosity, it would be shared with those "once-proud" nations who now lacked the means to travel into space. The brave cosmonauts who were reaping this harvest of riches were mentioned by name on several occasions. There was, of course, no word about how one of those brave cosmonauts had gone stark staring mad.

I knew with a cold certainty that they'd never tell the truth about Yakov. If he didn't recover they'd make something up—an unanticipated illness, or a debilitating accident. They'd kill the poor bastard rather than admit that we were human.

'I went to see him,' Galenka said, startling me. She had drifted into the recreation area quite silently. 'He's talking now—almost lucid. Want us to let him out of the module.'

'Not likely.'

'I agree. But we'll have to make a decision on him sooner or later.'

'Well, there's no hurry right now. You all right?'

'Fine, thanks.'

She had rested less than three hours, but in weightlessness—even after an exhausting task—that was enough. It was a useful physiological adaptation when there was a lot of work to be done, but it also meant that ten days in space could feel like thirty back on Earth. Or a hundred.

'Go and sleep some more, you want to. The Progress calls in, I'll wake you.'

'If it calls in.'

I offered a shrug. 'You did everything that was expected of you. That we got this far ...'

'I know; we should be very proud of ourselves.' She stared at the screen, her eyes still sleepy.

'They're going to lie about Yakov.'

'I know.'

'When we get home, they'll make us stick to the story.'

'Of course.' She said this with total resignation, as if it was the least any of us could expect.

Soon we bored of the news and the television. While Galenka was answering letters from friends and family I went back to run my own check on Yakov. To our disappointment Baikonur still had no specific recommendations beyond maintaining the present medication. I sensed that they didn't want blood on their hands if something went wrong with him. They were happy to let us take responsibility for our ailing comrade, even if we ended up killing him.

'Let me out, Dimitri. I'm fine now.'

I looked at him through the armoured glass of the bulkhead door. Shaking my head, I felt like a doctor delivering some dreadful diagnosis.

'You have to stay there for now. I'm sorry. But we can't run the risk of you trying to open the hatch again.'

'I accept that this isn't a simulation now. I accept that we're really in space.' His voice came through a speaker grille, tinny and distant. 'You believe me, don't you Dimitri?'

'I'll see you later, Yakov.'

'At least let me talk to Baikonur.'

I placed the palm of my hand against the glass. 'Later, friend. For now, get some rest.'

I turned away before he could answer.

He wasn't the only one who needed sleep. Tiredness hit me unexpectedly—it always came on hard, like a wall. I slept for two hours, dreaming of being back on Earth on a warm spring day, sitting with my wife in the park, the mission happily behind me, deemed a success by all concerned. When I woke the dream's melancholic after-effects dogged my thoughts for hours. I badly wanted to get home.

I found Galenka in the pilot's position.

'We have contact,' she said, but I knew from her tone of voice that it wasn't all good news.

'The Progress called in?'

'She's stuck, Dimitri. Jammed in down there. Can't back out, can't go forward.'

'Fuck.'

What was only apparent when the Progress reached the root complex was that there was no solid surface to Shell 4; that the tangled mass of roots was, to all intents and purposes, the sphere itself. There were gaps in that tangle, too, like the interstices in a loosely bundled ball of string. Methodically and fearlessly, the Progress had set about finding a way through to whatever was underneath. On its first attempt, it had travelled no more than a third of a kilometre beneath the nominal surface before reaching a narrowing it couldn't pass through. The second attempt, picking a different entry point, had taken it a kilometre under the surface before it met a similar impasse. With fuel now running low—just enough to get it back to the *Tereshkova*, with some in reserve—the Progress had opted to make one final attempt. It was then that it had got itself stuck, lodging in a part of the thicket like a bullet in gristle.

Galenka sent commands to the Progress, to be relayed when a window opened. She told it to use its manipulators to try and push itself backwards, and to wiggle its reaction thrusters in the hope that it might shake itself loose. It was the best she could do, but she wasn't optimistic. We waited three hours, by which time Baikonur were fully appraised of the situation. Then a window opened and the Progress reported that it was still jammed tight, despite executing Galenka's instructions.

'Before you say I should have listened to you,' she said. 'I did listen. But bringing her back in just wasn't the right decision, given what I knew at the time.'

'I fully concurred, Galenka. No one's blaming you.'

'Let's see what Baikonur have to say when we get back, shall we?'

'I'm sure they'll be in a forgiving mood. The amount of data we've gathered…'

'Doesn't begin to add up against physical samples, which we've now lost.'

'Maybe.'

'Maybe what? I've tried everything in the book. I know what that Progress can do, Dimitri. It isn't an escape artist.'

'We do have the Soyuz,' I said.

'We need it to take us home. Anyway, the Soyuz isn't rigged for remote control or sampling.'

'I wasn't thinking of remote control. I was thinking, we fly the Soyuz all the way in. It's the same size as the Progress, right? It has similar capabilities?'

'Give or take.' Her tone told me she wasn't exactly signing up for my idea with enthusiasm. 'And then what?'

'We reach the Progress, or get as close to it as we can without getting ourselves stuck. Then we EVA. It's a microgravity environment so we should be able to move around without too much difficulty. It'll be too risky to attempt to free the Progress, but there's nothing to stop us transferring the artefacts. Plenty of room aboard the Soyuz, to bring them back to the *Tereshkova*.'

She breathed heavily, as if she'd just come off the exercise cycle. 'This wasn't planned for. This wasn't in the book. No one ever mentioned going in with the Soyuz.'

'It was always an unstated option. Why do you think they sent us out here, Galenka? To operate the

Progress in real-time? Part of the reason, certainly, but not all of it.'

'It's too dangerous.'

'It was, but now we've got a much clearer picture of what's inside Shell 3. We can load in the Progress's trajectory and follow it all the way in.'

'And if we damage the Soyuz? It's a fiery ride home without it.'

'Why should we? We'll be taking excellent care of it.'

'Because our lives will depend on it. You've become very courageous all of a sudden, Dimitri. Don't take this the wrong way, but it's not what I expected of you.'

'I'm not trying to be anyone's hero. My blood's running cold at the idea of flying the Soyuz into that thing. But I happen to know the way their minds work back in Baikonur. They'll have thought of the Soyuz option by now, realised that it's feasible.'

'They won't force us to do it, though.'

'No, that's not how they operate. But if we don't raise the possibility, if we don't put it on the table, they'll be very, very disappointed. More disappointed than they'll already be at us for losing the robot.'

I watched her reflect on what I'd said. In this instance Galenka would have no option but to admit that my grasp of Baikonur politics was superior to hers. I had been a cosmonaut for longer and I had seen how our superiors punished failings. The best you could hope for was incarceration. The worst was returning to your office to find a bottle of vodka and a loaded revolver.

'I hope you're right about this, Dimitri. For both our sakes.'

'We have no choice,' I said. 'Trust me, Galenka. Nothing that happens in the Matryoshka will be as bad as what they'd do to us for failing our country.'

An hour later we'd informed Baikonur of our decision. Two hours later we had their reply. I went to Yakov and told him what was going to happen.

'You can let me out now,' he said, through the bulkhead window.

'Not until we're back.'

'You still don't trust me?'

'It's just not a risk we can afford to take.'

'Don't leave me alone on the *Tereshkova*. I'd rather go with you than stay here on my own.'

'Not an option, I'm afraid. We need the extra space in the Soyuz. But I'm opening comms to your module. You'll be able to talk to Baikonur, and you'll be able to talk to us. You won't feel out of touch.'

'I'm all right now,' Yakov said. 'Please believe me. I had a bad turn, I got confused—but everything's all right now.'

'I'm sorry.'

An hour after that, we were checking our suits and prepping the Soyuz for departure.

⊖⊖

'I need bread,' Nesha says. 'Let's go for a walk.'

'In this weather?'

'I need bread. If I don't go early, there'll be none left.'

I peer through the window, at the grey-white sky. 'I could fetch it for you. If you gave me some money, and told me where to go.' Seeing the sceptical look on her face, I add: 'I'd come back.'

'We'll go together. It's good exercise for me, to get out of this place. If I didn't have errands, I'd probably never leave the building.'

Nesha puts on several more layers of clothes and fetches a coat for herself. None of Gennadi's coats fit me (they're all too tight in the sleeves) so I'm forced to make do with Doctor Kizim's again. At least it's dried a bit, and I have something warm on underneath it. Nesha locks her apartment, turning keys in three separate locks, then we walk slowly to the elevator, still where I left it, on the ninth floor.

'I shouldn't have mocked you, Dimitri Ivanov.'

The elevator doors close. 'Mocked me?'

'About the musical box. The thing you came to give me. Now that we've spoken a little more, I see that you're not the mad man I thought you might be. I should have known better.'

'It's understandable.'

'Did it really come from the Matryoshka?'

'All the way back.'

'Why did they let you keep it?'

'Because they didn't realise its significance. By the time we got back, I knew that we weren't going to get an easy ride. The truth that we'd discovered—it wasn't

— 14 —

going to be something our political masters wanted to hear. We were all ill—the perfect excuse for incarceration in some nameless medical facility cum prison or madhouse. Yakov and Galenka were sick with radiation exposure. I was sick with the Matryoshka inside my head. None of us were going to see daylight again.'

'I read the papers and saw the television reports. They never actually lied about what happened to you.'

'They didn't have to. As long as there was a reason not to have us out in public, they were happy.'

The elevator completes its trundling, hesitant descent. We leave the building, venturing into the snow-covered street. I remain vigilant for prowling Zils and men in dark suits.

'I kept the musical box with me all the way home. When they found it they assumed it was one of my personal effects—something I'd taken aboard the ship when we left. The idea that it might be an *artefact*, a thing from the Matryoshka, never crossed their minds.'

'And you never thought to tell them?'

'They'd have destroyed it. So I kept it close with me, all the time I was in the facility. The only person I ever showed it to was Doctor Kizim, and I don't think even he believed where it had come from.'

'You must have trusted him.'

'You had to trust someone in a place like that. Just like I'm trusting you now. The musical box is yours now. It's a piece of the future, in your hands.'

She removes it from her coat. Until then I have no idea that she's brought it with her.

'The tune it makes…' She starts turning the little handle, the notes tinkling out. We're in the street, but there's no one else around to notice one old woman with a little metal box in her hands, or to question why she's turning the handle in its side. 'I think I know it. It's something familiar, isn't it? Something Russian?'

'Like you always said. But please don't play it now. It makes my head hurt.'

She stops turning the handle and returns the musical box to her pocket. We trudge on in silence until we're in sight of the shopping complex where Nesha hopes to find her bread. Dingy and disused as it appears, people are already milling around outside. Their dark winter clothes reduce them to an amorphous, weary mass. Our premier smiles down from the looming side of an apartment tower, lips moving but no sound coming out. Seagulls have been attracted by the flickering colours, pecking away huge pieces of his face.

'If the musical box was in the Matryoshka, then I was right about its origin,' Nesha says. 'It did come from the future after all.'

'They never believed you. They never wanted to believe you.'

She glances up at the birdshit-stained edifice, the premier's moving face. 'We live in a flawless collectivised utopia. But a flawless society can't, by definition, evolve. If it proceeds from one state to another, there must have been something wrong, or sub-optimal, about it. If it gets worse, then the seeds of that worsening must have already been present. It it gets better, than it has room for improvement. The mere fact that the future is not the same as the present ... that's totally unacceptable.'

'It all ends,' I say, keeping my voice low. 'In less than a human lifetime. That's what I learned inside the Matryoshka. That and the fact that you were right all along.'

'The musical box won't make any difference.'

'Except now you know.'

'There was never any doubt in my mind. Not even in the darkest days, when they punished me through Gennadi.' Nesha walks on a few paces. 'But still. It was always only a hypothesis. To have firm proof that I was right ... it does make a difference, to me.'

'That's all I ever wanted. I felt that we owed you that much. I'm just sorry it took me so long to reach you.'

'You did your best, Dimitri. You got to me in the end.' Then she reaches into her pocket again and takes out the change she's saved for the bread.

⊖⊖

'Clear,' I called from the porthole, as we undocked. 'Five meters. Ten metres. Fifteen.' The rest of the ship came into view, silvery under its untidy-looking quilt of reflective foil. It was a bittersweet moment. I'd been looking forward to getting this view for months, but I'd always assumed it would be at mission's end, as we were about to ride the Soyuz back into Earth's atmosphere.

'Lining us up,' Galenka said. She was in the command seat, wearing her EVA suit but with the helmet and gloves not yet in place.

I felt the Soyuz wheel around me as it orientated itself towards the Matryoshka. We'd be following the Progress all the way in, relying on the same collision-avoidance algorithm that had worked so well before. I kept telling myself that there was no reason for it to stop working now, just because we were aboard, but I couldn't quell my fears. My nerves had been frayed even when it had just been the robot at stake. I kept thinking of that American probe sliced in two, coming apart in two perfectly severed halves. How would it feel, I wondered, if we ran into one of those infinitely-sharp field lines? Would we even notice it at first? Would there even be pain, or just a sudden cold numbness from half our bodies?

As it was, we sailed through Shell 1 and Shell 2 without incident. All the while we remained in contact with the *Tereshkova*, and all the while the *Tereshkova* remained in contact with the microsat swarm. As windows opened and closed in Shell 3, the Progress reported on its continued existence and functionality. Nothing had happened to it since our departure. It was stuck, but otherwise operational and undamaged.

I clutched at every crumb of comfort. The Matryoshka hadn't touched the robot. It hadn't shown any sign of having noticed it. Didn't that bode well for us? If it didn't object to one foreign object, there was no reason for it to object to another, especially if we took pains not to get stuck ourselves.

Galenka brought us to a hovering standstill above Shell 3. In the microgravity environment of the Matryoshka, the Soyuz only needed to exert a whisper of thrust from its attitude motors to hold station.

'You'd better get buckled in, Dimitri. When a window opens, I'm giving her the throttle. It'll feel like a booster separation, only harder.'

I made sure I was tight in my seat. 'I'm ready. How long do you think?'

'No idea. Just be ready for it when it comes.'

The glass cockpit of the Soyuz was much more advanced than the basic frame of the ship itself, which was older than my grandmother. Before our departure, Galenka had configured the sensors and readouts to emulate the same telemetry she'd been seeing from the Progress. Now all she had to do was watch the scrolling, chattering indications for the auguries of an opening window. She'd have no more than a second or two to assess whether it was a window she could reach in time, given the Soyuz's capabilities. Deciding that there was nothing I could contribute to the matter, I closed my eyes and waited for the moment.

No matter what happened now, we had made history. We were inside the Matryoshka—the first humans to have made it this far. It had taken three apparitions to achieve this feat. Once, it had seemed axiomatic that things would only go from strength to strength with each return. By the time of the fourth apparition, it seemed inconceivable that there would not be a permanent human presence out here, following the Matryoshka throughout its orbit. Study stations, research facilities—an entire campus, floating in vacuum.

I wondered now if anyone would come after us. The space effort was winding down—even the *Tereshkova* was cobbled together from the bits of earlier, failed enterprises. It seemed to me—though I would never have voiced such a conviction publically—that it was less important to my country what we found out here, than that we were seen to be doing something no one else could. The scientific returns were almost incidental. Next time, would anyone even bother sending out a ship?

'Brace,' Galenka said.

The thrust was a hoof kick to the spine. It was worst than any booster separation, stage ignition or de-orbit burn. I had experienced re-entry gee-loads that were enough to push me to the brink of unconsciousness, but those forces had built up slowly, over several minutes. This came instantly, and for a moment I felt as if no bone in my body could possibly have survived unbroken.

Then I realised that I was all right. The engine was still burning, but at least the gee-load was a steady pressure now, like a firm hand rather than a fist.

'We are good for insertion,' Galenka said, as if that had ever been in doubt.

We sailed through the two closely-packed shells, into the luminous blue-green interstitial space above Shell 4. Once we were clear—with the window sealing above us—Galenka did a somersault roll to use the main engine to slow us down again. The thrust burst was longer and less brutal this time. She dropped our speed from hundreds of metres per second to what was only slightly faster than walking pace. The thicket lay ahead or below, depending on my mental orientation. We were making good time. There was no need to rush things now.

Maybe, just maybe, we'd get away with this.

A screen flashed red and began scrolling with error messages. 'There goes the *Tereshkova*,' Galenka said. 'We're out of contact now.' She gave me a fierce grin. 'Just you and me, and an impenetrable shell of alien matter between us and the outside world. Starting to feel claustrophobic yet?'

'I'd be insane not to. Do we have a fix on the Progress?'

She jabbed a finger at another readout—target cross-hairs against a moving grid. 'Dead ahead, where she said she was. Judging by the data she recorded before getting stuck, we'll be able to get within two hundred metres without difficulty. I won't risk taking the Soyuz any closer, but we should be able to cover the remaining distance in suits.'

'Whatever it takes.' I checked my watch, strapped around the sleeve of my suit. We'd been out from the mother ship for less than three and a half hours—well ahead of schedule. We had air and fuel to spare, but I still wanted to be out of here as quickly as possible. 'How soon until we're in position?' I asked.

'Twenty minutes, give or take.'

'We spend two hours on station. Nothing changes that. If we don't succeed in unloading everything, we still leave. Are we clear on that?'

'This was your idea, Dimitri. You decide when we leave.'

'I'm going to finish suiting up. We'll check comms and life-support thoroughly before we leave. And we'll make damned sure the Soyuz isn't going to drift away from us.'

Galenka's estimate was on the nail. Twenty minutes later we were deep into the thicket, with blue-green structures crowding around us. Closest to us was a trunk or branch with thornlike protrusions. Galenka brought the Soyuz in against the trunk until the hull shuddered with the contact. Ordinarily I'd have been worried about a pressure rupture, but now that we were both wearing helmets that was only a distant concern. Galenka had picked her spot well, the Soyuz resting on one of the out-jutting thorns. Friction, and the ship's almost negligible weight, would serve to hold it in place until we were ready to leave. Galenka had even taken to pains to make sure the forward escape hatch was not blocked.

'Maybe you should stay here, while I check out the Progress,' I said. I didn't feel heroic, but it seemed the right thing to say.

'If we have to unload it, it'll go quicker with two of us,' Galenka responded. 'We can form a supply chain, save going all the way back each time. And keep an eye on each other.' She unbuckled. 'You ready for this? I'm going to vent our air.'

She let the air drain out through the release valve before opening the hatch. My suit ballooned around me, the seals and joints creaking with the pressure differential. I'd checked everything, but I was all too conscious of the thin membranes of fabric protecting me from lung-freezing death. Every gesture, every movement, was now more awkward, more potentially hazardous than before. Tear a glove on sharp metal, and you might as well have cut your hand off.

Galenka popped the hatch. I pushed these concerns from my mind and exited the Soyuz. Now that I was seeing the alien environment with my own eyes—through a thin glass visor, rather than a thick porthole or monitor—it appeared not only larger, but vastly more oppressive and strange. The all-enveloping shell was a pitiless, hope-crushing black. I told myself that a window would eventually open for us to leave, just as one had allowed us to enter. But it was hard to shake the feeling that we were little warm animals, little shivering mammals with fast heartbeats, caught in a cold dark trap that we had just sprung.

'Let's do this shit, and get back home,' Galenka said, pushing past me.

We climbed down the pea-green flank of the Soyuz, using the handholds that had been bolted on for weightless operations. We left the ship with the hatch open, the last dribbles of air still venting from the hull. My feet touched the thorn. Although I had almost no weight to speak of, the surface felt solid under me. It was formed from the same translucent material as the rest of Shell 4, but it wasn't as slippery as glass or ice. I reached out a hand and steadied myself against the trunk. I felt as if I was touching bark or rock through my glove.

'I think we can do this,' I said.

'The Progress should be directly under us, where this trunk constricts against the one over here. I'd rather climb than drift, if that's OK with you.'

'Agreed. There are thorns all the way down, spaced every three or four meters—we should be able to use them for grabs, even if we can't get traction on the rest of it. It shouldn't be much harder coming back up.'

'I'm right behind you.'

If the thicket registered our presence, there was no evidence of it. The structure loomed around us, dizzying in its scale and complexity, but giving no sign of being alive or responsive to the intrusion of human technology. I began to ease, trying to imagine myself in a forest or cave system—something huge but mindless—rather than the glowing guts of an alien machine.

It took fifteen minutes of cautious progress to reach the lodged Progress. It was jammed in nose first, with the engine pointing-at us. A ship like that was not normally a man-rated vehicle, but the usual variants had a hatch at the front, so that space station crews could enter the vehicle when it was docked. Our Progress had been augmentd with scientific gear, computers, additional fuel and batteries. The docking hatch had become a kind of mouth by which the robot could feed samples into itself, using the feeler-like appendages of its sampling devices. Inside was a robotic system which sorted the samples, fed them into miniature laboratories where appropriate, and delivered whatever was left into a storage volume just ahead of the fuel tanks. We couldn't have got in through the mouth even if the Progress hadn't been jammed in nose first, but that didn't matter. A secondary hatch and docking assembly had been installed in the side, so that the sample compartment could be unloaded through the *Tereshkova*'s own docking port. Galenka, who had overtaken me in our descent from the Soyuz, was the first to reach the sample hatch. The controls were designed to be opened by someone in a suit. She worked the heavy toggles until the hatch swung open, exposing the non-pressurised storage compartment. The hole in the side of the Progress was just large for a suited person to crawl through. Without hesitation she grabbed yellow handholds and levered herself inside. A few moments later the chamber lit up with the wavering light of her helmet-mounted flashlamp.

'Talk to me, Galenka.'

'It's all racked and sorted, Dimitri. Must be about half a tonne of stuff in here already. Some of the chunks are pretty big. Still warm, too. Going to be a bitch of a job moving all of them back to the Soyuz.'

'We'll take what we can; that was always the idea. If nothing else we should make sure we've got unique samples from both Shell 1 and Shell 2.'

'I'm going to try and bring out the first chunk. I'll pass it through the hatch. Be ready.'

'I'm here.'

But as I said that, a status panel lit up on the side of my faceplate. 'Comms burst from *Tereshkova*,' I said, as alphanumeric gibberish scrolled past. 'A window must just have opened.'

'Feeling better now?'

'Guess it's nice to know the windows are still behaving.'

'I could have told you they would.' Galenka grunted with the effort of dislodging the sample she had selected. 'So—any news?'

'Nothing. Just a carrier signal, trying to establish contact with us. Means the ship's still out there, though.'

'I could have told you that as well.'

It took twenty minutes to convey one sample back to the Soyuz. Doing it as a relay didn't help—it took two of us to nurse the object between us, all the while making sure we didn't drift away from the structure. Things got a little faster after that. We returned to the jammed Progress in good time and only took fifteen minutes to get the second sample back to our ship. We now had pieces of Shell 1 and Shell 2 aboard, ready to be taken back home.

A voice at the back of my head said that we should quit while we were ahead. We'd salvaged something from this mess—almost certainly enough to placate Baikonur. We had taken a risk and it had paid off. But there was still more than an hour remaining of the time I had allowed us. If we moved quickly and efficiently—and we were already beginning to settle into a rhythm—we could recover three or four additional samples before it was time to start our journey back. Who knew what difference five or six samples might make, compared to two?

'Just for the record,' Galenka said, when we reached the Progress again, 'I'm getting itchy feet here.'

'We've still got time. Two more. Then we'll see how we're doing.'

'You were a lot more jumpy until that window opened.'

She was right. I couldn't deny it.

I was thinking of that when another comms burst came through. For a moment I was gladdened—just seeing the scroll of numbers and symbols, even if it meant nothing to me, made me feel closer to the *Tereshkova*. Home was just three shells and a sprint across vacuum away. Almost close enough to touch, like the space station that had sped across the sky over Klushino, when my father held me on his shoulders.

'Dimitri,' crackled a voice. 'Galenka. Yakov here. I hope you can hear me.'

'What is it, friend?' I asked, hearing an edge in his voice I didn't like.

'You'd better listen carefully—we could get cut off at any moment. Baikonur detected a change in the Matryoshka—a big one. Shell 1 pulsations have increased in amplitude and frequency. It's like nothing anyone's seen since the first apparition. Whatever you two are doing in there—it's having an effect. The thing is waking. You need to think about getting out, while the collision-avoidance algorithm will still get you through Shell 1. Those pulsations change any more, the algorithm won't be any use.'

'He could be lying,' Galenka said. 'Saying whatever he needs to say that get us to go back.'

'I'm not lying. I want you to come back. And I want that Soyuz back so that at least one of us can get home.'

'I think we'd better move,' I said.

'The remaining samples?'

'Leave them. Let's just get back to the ship as quickly as possible.'

As I spoke, the comms window blipped out. Galenka pushed away from the Progress. I levered myself onto the nearest thorn and started climbing. It was quicker now that we didn't have to carry anything between us. I thought of the changing conditions in Shell 1 and hoped that we'd still be able to pick a path through the lethal, shifting maze of field-lines.

We were half way to the Soyuz—I could see it overhead, tantalising near—when Galenka halted, only just below me.

'We're in trouble,' she said.

'What?'

'Look down, Dimitri. Something's coming up.'

I followed her instruction and understood. We couldn't see the Progress any more. It was lost under a silver tide, a sea of gleaming mercury climbing slowly through the thicket, swallowing everything as it rose.

'Climb,' I said.

'We're not going to make it, Dimitri. It's rising too quickly.'

I gritted my teeth: typical Galenka, pragmatic to the end. But even she had resumed her ascent, unable to stop her body from doing what her mind knew to be futile. She was right, too. The tide was going to envelope us long before we reached the Soyuz. But I couldn't stop climbing either. I risked a glance down and saw the silver fluid lapping at Galenka's heels, then surging up to swallow her lowest boot.

'It's got me.'

'Keep moving.'

She pulled the boot free, reached the next thorn, and for a moment it appeared that she might be capable of out-running the fluid. My mind raced ahead to the Soyuz, realising that even if we got there in time, even if we got inside and sealed the hatch, we wouldn't be able to get the ship aloft in time.

Then the fluid took more of Galenka. It lapped to her thighs, then her waist. She slowed her climb.

'It's pulling me back,' she said, grunting with the effort. 'It's trying to drag me in.'

'Fight it.'

Maybe she did—it was hard to tell, with her movements so impeded. The tide consumed her to the chest, taking her backpack, then absorbed her helmet. She had one hand raised above her head, grasping for the next thorn. The tide took it.

'Galenka.'

'I'm here.' She came through indistinctly, comms crackling with static. 'I'm in it now. I can't see anything. But I can still move, still breathe. It's like being in the immersion tank.'

'Try and keep climbing.'

'Picking up some suit faults now. Fluid must be interfering with the electronics, with the cooling system.' She faded out, came back, voice crazed with pops and crackles and hisses. 'Oh, God. It's inside. I can feel it. It's cold, against my skin. Rising through the suit. How the fuck did it get in?'

She faded.

'Galenka. Talk to me.'

'In my helmet now. Oh, God. Oh, God. It's still rising. I'm going to drown, Dimitri. This is not right. I did not want to fucking *drown*.'

'Galenka?'

I heard a choked scream, then a gurgle. Then nothing.

I kept climbing, while knowing it was useless. The tide reached me a few moments later. It swallowed me and then found a way into my suit, just as it had with Galenka.

Then it found a way into my head.

ᘖᘗ

We didn't drown.

There was a moment of absolute terror as it forced its way down my throat, through my eye sockets, nose and ears. The gag reflex kicked in, and then it was over. Not terror, no panic, just blissful unconsciousness.

Until I woke up on my back.

The silver tide was abating. It had left our bodies, left the inside of our suits. It was draining off them in chrome rivulets, leaving them dry and undamaged. We were lying like upended turtles, something like Earth-normal gravity pinning us to the floor. It took all my effort to lever myself into a sitting position, and then to stand up, fighting the weight of my backpack as it tried to drag me down. My suit was no longer ballooning out, meaning that we were in some kind of pressurised environment.

I looked around, taking deep, normal breaths.

Galenka and I were in a huge iron-grey room with gill-like sluice vents in the side walls. The fluid was rushing out through the vents, exposing a floor of slightly twinkling black, like polished marble. Grey-blue light poured down through hexagonal grids in the arched ceiling. I wasn't going to take any chances on it being breathable.

I inspected the outer covering for tears or abrasions, but it looked as good as when I'd worn it.

'Galenka,' I said. 'Can you hear me?'

'Loud and clear, Dimitri.' I heard her voice on the helmet radio, but also coming through the glass, muffled but comprehensible. 'Whatever we just went through—I don't think it hurt our suits.'

'Do you still have air?'

'According to the gauge, good for another six hours.'

'How do you feel?'

'Like I've been scrubbed inside with caustic soda. But otherwise—I'm all right. Clear-headed, like I've just woken up after a really slong sleep. I actually feel better, more alert, than before we left the Soyuz.'

'That's how I feel,' I said. 'Where do you think we are?'

'The heart of it. The middle of the Matryoshka. Where else could we be? It must have brought us here for a reason. Maybe it wants to assess the foreign objects it detected, then work out how best to recycle or dispose of them.'

'Maybe. But then why keep us alive? It must recognise that we're living. It must recognise that we're thinking beings.'

'Always the optimist, Dimitri.'

'Something's happening. Look.'

A bar of light had cut across the base of part of the wall. It was becoming taller, as if a seamless door was opening upwards. The light ramming through the widening gap was the same grey-blue that came through the ceiling. Both of us tensing, expecting to be squashed out of existence at any moment, we turned to face whatever awaited us.

Beyond was a kind of corridor, sloping down in a gently steepening arc, so that the end was not visible except as an intensification of that silvery glow. The inwardly-sloping walls of the corridor—rising to a narrow spine of a ceiling—were dense with intricately carved details, traced in the blue-grey light.

'I think we should walk,' Galenka said, barely raising her voice above a whisper.

We started moving, taking stiff, slow paces in our EVA suits. We passed through the door, into the corridor. We commenced down the curved ramp of the floor. Though I should have been finding it harder and harder to keep my footing, I had no sense that I was on a steepening grade. I looked at Galenka and she was still walking upright, at right angles to the surface of the floor. I paused to turn around, but already the room we had been in was angled out of view, with the door beginning to lower back down.

'Do you hear that sound?' Galenka asked.

I had been about to say the same thing. Over the huff and puff of our suit circulators it was not the easiest thing to make out. But there was a low droning noise, like the bass note of an organ. It was coming from all around us, from the very fabric of the Matryoshka. It sustained a note for many seconds before changing pitch. As we walked we heard a pattern of notes repeat, with subtle variations. I couldn't piece together the tune, if indeed there was one—it too slow, too deep for that—but I didn't think I was hearing the random emanations of some mindless mechanical process.

'It's music,' I said. 'Slowed down almost to death. But it's still music.'

'Look at the walls, Dimitri.'

They were astonishing. The walls had been carved with a hypnotically detailed mazelike pattern, one that I could never quite bring into focus. Edges and ridges of the pattern pushed out centimetres from the wall. I felt a strange impulse to reach out and touch, as if there was a magnetic attraction working on my fingers.

Even as I acknowledged this impulse, Galenka—walking to my left—reached out her left hand and skirted the pattern on her side. She flinched and withdrew her gloved fingers with a gasp of something that could have been pain or astonishment or simple childlike delight.

'What?' I asked.

'I just got … I can't describe it, Dimitri. It was like—everything.'

'Everything what?'

'Everything trying to get into my head. Everything at once. Like the whole universe gatecrashing my brain. It wasn't unpleasant. It was just—too much.'

I reached out my hand.

'Be careful.'

I touched the wall. Knowledge, clean and viridescent, as brittle and endlessly branching as a flower chilled in liquid nitrogen, forced its way into my skull. I felt mental sutures straining under the pressure. I flinched back, just as Galenka had done. The contact could not have lasted more than an instant, but the information that had gushed through was ringing in my skull like the after-chime of God's own church bell.

A window of comprehension had opened and slammed shut again. I was dizzy with what it had shown me. I already knew more about the Matryoshka than any other living person, with the possible exception of Galenka.

'It's come from the future,' I said.

'I got that as well.'

'They sent it here. They sent it here to carry a message to us.'

I knew these things with an unimpeachable certainty, but I had no additional context for the knowledge. What future, by whom? From how far ahead, and to what purpose? What message? How had it arrived?

I couldn't stand not knowing. Now that I knew part of the truth, I needed the rest.

I reached out my hand again, caressed the wall. It hit me harder this time, but the instinct to flinch away, the instinct to close my mind, was not as strong. I gasped at the crystalline rush. There couldn't be room in my head for all that was being pumped into it, and yet it continued without interruption. Layers of wisdom poured into me, cooling and stratifying like ancient rock. My head felt like a boulder perched on my shoulders. I laughed: it was the only possible response, other than screaming terror. The flow continued, increasing in pressure.

This much I understood:

The Matryoshka was a complex machine with a simple purpose. Its layered structure was borne of necessity; the way it had to be in order to complete its mission. Each layer was a form of armour or camouflage or passkey, evolved organically to enable it to slip through the threshing clockwork of a cosmic time machine. That time machine was older than Earth. It had been constructed by alien minds and then added to and modified by successive intelligences. It was as far beyond the Matryoshka as the Matryoshka was beyond the Soyuz.

The time machine had been waiting in a state of dormancy, for more than a billion years. Then humanity, or what had become of humanity, chanced upon it.

It took a little while to understand its nature.

At its ticking, whirling core lay a necklace of neutron stars. It had been known since our own era that a sufficiently long, dense, and fast-rotating cylinder had the property of twisting spacetime around itself until a path into the past became possible. Such a path—a mathematical trajectory in space, like an orbit—offered a means of conveying a signal or object to any previous point in time, provided it was no earlier than the moment of the time machine's construction.

Constructing such a machine was anything but child's play.

A single neutron star could be made to have the requisite density and spin, but it lacked the necessary axial elongation. To overcome this, the machine's builders had approximated a cylinder by stringing four hundred and forty-one neutron stars together until they were almost touching, like beads on a wire. An open-ended string would have collapsed under its own appalling self-gravity, so the ends had been bent around and joined, with the entire ensemble revolving fast enough to stabilise the neutron stars against falling inward. It still wasn't a cylinder, but locally—as far as a photon or vehicle near the necklace was concerned—it might as well have been.

If it had taken a while to understand the time machine, it had taken even longer to engineer a vehicle capable of traversing it. The construction of the Matryoshka was the last great enterprise of a waning civilisation.

The machine had catapulted the Matryoshka into the prehuman past of our galaxy. The insertion into time-reversed flight, the passage through the various filters and barriers installed to prevent illicit use of the ancient machinery, the exit back into normal timeflow, had caused eleven additional layers of shell to be sacrificed. What we saw of the Matryoshka was merely the scarred kernel of what had once been a much larger entity.

But it had survived. It had come through, albeit overshooting its target era by many millions of years. Yet that had been allowed for; it was easier to leap back into the deep past and crawl forward in time than to achieve a bullseye into a relatively recent era. The emergence event was indeed the opening of a local wormhole throat, but only so that the Matryoshka (which incorporated wormhole-manipulating machinery in Shells 1 and 2) could complete the last leg of its journey.

How far downstream had it come? A hundred years? A thousand years? Five thousand?

I couldn't tell. The knowledge told me everything, but not all of that wisdom was framed in terms I could readily decode. But I could sense a thread, a sense of connectedness between the era of the Matryoshka and our own. They knew a lot about us.

Enough to know that we were on the wrong path.

At last I jerked my hand away from the wall. The urge to return it was almost overwhelming, but I could only take so much in one go.

'Dimitri?'

'I'm here.'

'I thought you were gone for a while there.'

I turned to face my comrade. Against the vastness I had been shown, the cosmic scale of the history I had almost glimpsed, Galenka appeared no more substantial than a paper cut-out. She was just a human being, translucent with her own insubstantiality, pinned in this one moving instant like dirt on a conveyor belt. It took moments for my sense of scale to normalise; to realise that, for all that the machine had shown me, I was no different.

'They sent it back for us,' I said. The words came out in a rush, and yet at the same time each syllable consumed an eternity of time and effort. 'To show us how we've gone wrong. There's history here—lots of it. In these walls. Mountains, chasms, of data.'

'You need to slow your breathing. That silver stuff that got into us—it's primed us in some way, hasn't it? Rewired our minds so that the Matryoshka can get into them?'

'I think—maybe. Yes.'

'Get a grip, Dimitri. We still need to get home.'

I made to touch the wall again. The urge was still there, the hunger—the vacuum in my head—returning. The Matryoshka still had more to tell me. It was not done with Dimitri Ivanov.

'Don't,' Galenka said, with a firmness that stopped my hand. 'Not now. Not until we've seen the rest of this place.

At her urging I resisted. I found that if kept to the middle of the corridor, it wasn't as bad. But the walls were still whispering to me, inviting me to stroke my hand against them.

'The Second Soviet,' I said.

'What about it?'

'It falls. Fifty years from now, maybe sixty. Somewhere near the end of the century. I saw it in the history.' I paused and swallowed hard. 'This road we're on—this path. It's not the right one. We took a wrong turn, somewhere between the first and second apparitions. But by the time we realise it, by the time the Soviet falls, it's too late. Not just for Russia, but for Earth. For humankind.'

'It came from our future. Even I felt that, and I only touched it briefly. If we sent it, then things can't be all bad.'

'It's the wrong future,' I said. 'The Matryoshka is almost the last thing they do. They've been on the wrong path, doomed, from the outset. We turned away from space—that's the mistake. There's a darkness between then and now, and when it comes we aren't ready.'

We were still walking, following the arcing downslope of the corridor, towards the silver-blue radiance at its end. 'The Second Soviet is the only political organisation still doing space travel. If anything we're the ones holding the candle.'

'It's not enough. Now that the other nations have abandoned their efforts, we have to do more than just subsist. And if we are holding the candle, it won't be for much longer.'

'I don't understand how the choices we make here and now can make that much of a difference, however many years from now.'

'Evidently they can, or our descendants wouldn't have gone to all this trouble. Look, we're both smart enough to understand that small changes in initial conditions can feed into a chaotic system in highly unpredictable ways. What is history but a chaotic system?'

'The Second Soviet won't like being told it's a mistake of history, Dimitri.'

There was a fierce dryness in my throat. 'It can't ignore the message in the Matryoshka. Not now.'

'I wouldn't be too sure about that. But you know something?'

'What?'

'If this thing is from the future—from our future—then maybe it's Russian as well. Or sent back to meet Russians. Which might mean that Nesha Petrova was right after all.'

'They should tell her.'

'I'm sure it'll be the first thing on their minds, after they've spent all these years crushing and humiliating her.' Galenka fell silent for a few paces. 'It's like they always knew, isn't it.'

'They couldn't have.'

'But they knew enough to want her to be wrong. A message from the future, intended for us? What could *we* possibly need to hear from our descendants, except their undying gratitude?'

'Everything we say is being logged on our suit recorders,' I said. 'Logged and compressed and stored, so that it can be sent back to the Soyuz and then back to the *Tereshkova*, and then back to Baikonur.'

'Right now, comrade, there are few things I give less of a damn about than some arsehole of a party official listening to what I have to say.'

I smiled, because that was exactly how I felt as well.

In sixty years the Second Soviet was dust. The history I had absorbed told me that nothing could prevent that. Accelerate it, yes—and maybe the arrival of the Matryoshka would do just that—but not prevent it. They could crucify us and it wouldn't change anything.

It was a crumb of consolation.

The corridor widened, the intricate walls flanking away on either side, until we reached a domed room of cathedral proportions. The chamber was round, easily a hundred metres across, with a domed ceiling. I saw no way in or out other than the way we had come. There was a jagged design in the floor, worked in white and black marble—rapier-thin shards radiating from the middle.

The music intensified—rising in pitch, rising in speed. If there was a tune there it was almost on the point of being comprehensible. I had a mental image of a rushing winter landscape, under white skies.

'This is it, then,' Galenka said. 'An empty fucking room. After all this.' She took a hesitant step towards the middle, then halted.

'Wait,' I said.

Something was happening.

The black and white shards were pulling back from the middle, sliding invisibly into the floor's circular border, a star-shaped blackness opening up in the centre. It all happened silently, with deathly slowness. Galenka stepped back, the two of us standing side by side. When the star had widened to ten or twelve metres across, the floor stopped moving. Smoothly, silently, something rose from the darkness. It was a plinth, and there was a figure on the plinth, lying with his face to the domed ceiling. Beneath the plinth, icy with frost, was a thick tangle of pipes and coiling, intestinal machinery. We stood and watched it in silence, neither of us ready to make the first move. There was a tingle in my head that was not quite a headache just now, but which promised to become one.

The floor began to slide back into place, the jagged blades locking into place beneath the plinth. There was now an uninterrupted surface between the resting figure and us. Galenka and I glanced at each other through our visors then began a slow, measured walk. The slope-sided plinth rose two metres from the floor, putting the reclining figure just above our heads. It hadn't moved, or shown the least sign of life, since emerging through the floor.

We reached the plinth. There was a kind of ledge or step in the side, allowing us to bring our heads level with the figure. We stood looking at it, saying nothing, the silence only punctuated by the laboured, bellows-like sound of our air circulators.

That it was human had been obvious from the moment the plinth rose. The shape of the head, the ribbed chest, the placement and articulation of the limbs—it was all too familiar to be alien. Anyway, I knew that something descended from us—something essentially human—had sent back the Matryoshka. My bright new memories told me now that I was seeing the pilot, the navigator that had steered the artefact through the vicious barbs of the booby-trapped time machine, and then up through time, skipping through a cascade of wormholes, to our present era. The pilot was ghostly pale, wraithe-thin and naked, lying on a white metallic couch or rack that at first glance appeared to be an apparatus of torture or savage restraint. But then I decided that the apparatus was merely the control and life-support interface for the pilot. It was what had kept him alive, and what had given him the reins of the vast, layered machine it was his duty to steer and safeguard.

I sensed that the journey had not been a short one. In the Matryoshka's reference frame, it had consumed centuries of subjective time. The pilot, bio-modified for longevity and uninterrupted consciousness, had experienced every howling second of his voyage. That had always been the intention.

But something had gone wrong. A miscalculation, a problem with the injection into the time machine. Or the emergence event, or the wormhole skip. Something I couldn't grasp, except in the nature of its outcome. The journey wasn't supposed to have taken this long.

'The pilot went mad.'

'You know this for a fact,' Galenka said.

'You'd think this was a punishment—to be put inside the Matryoshka, alone, hurled back in time. But in fact it was the highest honour imaginable. They glorified him. He was entrusted with a mission of unimaginable importance.'

'To change their past?'

'No. They were stuck with what they already had. You can change someone else's past, but not your own. That's how time travel works. We have a different future now—one that won't necessarily include the people who built the Matryoshka. But they did it for us, not themselves. To redeem one possible history, even if they couldn't mend their own. And he paid for that with his sanity.'

Galenka was silent for long moments. I surveyed the figure, taking in more of the details. Had he been standing, he would have towered over both of us. His arms were by his sides—his hands were small and boyish, out of proportion to the rest of him. His fists were clenched. The emaciated form was partly machine. The couch extended parts of itself into his body. Glowing blue lines slipped into orifices and punctured his flesh at a dozen points. Hard, non-biological forms bulged under drum-tight flesh. His eye sockets were stuffed with faceted blue crystals, radiating a spray of glowing fibres. There was something not quite right about the shape of his skull, as if some childhood deformity had never healed in the right way. It was hairless, papered over with translucent, finely veined skin. His lips were a bloodless gash.

'The music,' Galenka said, breaking the reverence. 'You think it's coming from his head, don't you.'

'I think music must have comforted him during his journey. Somewhere along the way, though, it swallowed him up. It's locked in a loop, endlessly repeating. He's like a rat in a wheel, going round and round. By the time he came out of the wormhole, there couldn't have been enough left of him to finish the mission.'

'He made the Matryoshka sing.'

'It might have been the last thing he did, before the madness took over completely. The last message he could get through to us. He knew how alien the artefact would have appeared to us, with its shells of camouflage and disguise. He made it sing, thinking we'd understand. A human signal, a sign that we shouldn't fear it. That no matter how alien it appeared on the outside, there was something human at the heart. A message for the species, a last chance not to screw things up.'

'Would it have killed him to use radio?'

'He had to get it through Shell 3, remember—not to mention how many shells we've come through since Shell 4. Maybe it just wasn't possible. Maybe the simplest thing really was to have the Matryoshka sing itself to us. After all, it's not as if someone didn't notice in the end.'

'Or maybe he was just insane, and the music's just a side-effect.'

'That's also a possibility,' I said.

The impulse that had drawn my hand towards the patterned wall compelled me to reach out and touch the pilot. I was moving my arm when the figure twitched, convulsing within the constraints of the couch. The blue lines strained like ropes in a squall. I jerked in my suit, nerves battling with curiosity. The figure was still again, but something about it had changed.

'Either it just died,' Galenka said, 'or it just came back to life. You want to take a guess, Dimitri?'

I said nothing. It was all I could do to stare at the pilot. His chest wasn't moving, and I doubted that there was a heart beating inside that ribcage. But something was different.

The pilot's head turned. The movement was glacially slow, more like a flower following the sun than the movement of an animal. It must have cost him an indescribable effort just to look at us. I could read no expression in the tight mask of his face or the blue facets of his eyes. But I knew we had his full attention.

The gash of his lips opened. He let out a long, slow sigh.

'You made it,' I said. 'You completed your mission.'

Perhaps it was my imagination—I would never know for certain—but it seemed to me then that the head nodded a fraction, as if acknowledging what I had said. As if thanking me for bringing this news.

Then there was another gasp of air—longer, this time. It had something of death about it. The eyes were still looking at me, but all of a sudden I sensed no intellect behind them. I wondered if the pilot had conserved some last flicker of sanity for the time when he had visitors— just enough selfhood to die knowing whether he had succeeded or failed.

Tension exited the body. The head lolled back into the frame, looking sideways. His arm slumped to the side, dangling over the side of the plinth. The fist relaxed, letting something small and metallic drop to the floor.

I reached down and picked up the item, taking it as gingerly I could in my suit gloves. I stared down at it as if it was the most alien thing in the universe. Which, in that moment, I think it probably was.

'A keepsake,' I said, wondering aloud. 'Something he was allowed to bring with him from the future. Something as ancient as the world he was aiming for. Something that must have been centuries old when he began his journey.'

'Maybe,' Galenka said.

I closed my own fist around the musical box. It was a simple human trinket, the most innocent of machines. I wanted to take my gloves off, to find out what it played. But I wondered if I already knew.

A little later the chrome tide came to wash us away again.

⋐⋑

The men are waiting next to Nesha's apartment when we return with her bread. I never saw their Zil, if that was how they arrived. There are three of them. They all have heavy black coats on, with black leather gloves. The two burlier men—whose faces mean nothing to me—have hats on, the brims dusted with snow. The third man isn't wearing a hat, although he has a pale blue scarf around his throat. He's thinner than the others, with a shaven, bullet-shaped head and small round glasses that bestow a look somewhere between professorial and ascetic. Something about his face is familiar: I feel that we've known each other somewhere before. He's taking a cigarette out of a packet when our eyes lock. It's the same contraband variety I used to buy my ride into town.

'This is my fault,' I say to Nesha. 'I didn't mean to bring these men here.'

'We've come to take you back to the facility,' the bald man says, pausing to ignite the cigarette from a miniature lighter. 'Quite frankly, I didn't expect to find you alive. I can't tell you what a relief it is to find you.'

'Do I know you?'

'Of course you know me. I'm Doctor Grechko. We've spent a lot of time together at the facility.'

'I'm not going back. You know that by now.'

'I beg to differ.' He takes a long drag on the cigarette. 'You're coming with us. You'll thank me for it eventually.' He nods at one of the hatted men, who reaches into his coat pocket and extracts a syringe with a plastic cap on the needle. The man pinches the cap between his gloved fingers and removes it. He holds the syringe to eye level, taps away bubbles and presses the plunger to squirt out a few drops of whatever's inside.

The railing along the balcony is very low. There's snow on the ground nine floors below, but it won't do much to cushion my fall. I've done what I came to do, so what's to prevent me from taking my own life, in preference to being taken back to the facility?

'I'm sorry I brought this on you,' I tell Nesha, and make to lift myself over the railing. My resolve at that moment is total. I'm surrendered to the fall, ready for white annihilation. I want the music in my head to end. Death and silence, for eternity.

But I'm not fast enough, or my resolve isn't as absolute as I imagine. The other hatted man rushes to me and locks his massive hand around my arm. The other one moves closer with the syringe.

'Not just yet,' Doctor Grechko—if that was his name—says. 'He's safe now, but keep a good grip on him.'

'What happens to Nesha?' I ask.

Grechko looks at her, then shakes his head. 'There's no harm in talking to a madwoman, Georgi. Whatever you may have told her, she'll confuse it with all that rubbish she already believes. No worse than telling secrets to a dog. And even if she didn't, no one would listen to her. Really, she isn't worth our inconvenience. You, on the other hand, are extraordinarily valuable to us.'

Something's wrong. I feel an icebreaker cutting through my brain.

'My name isn't Georgi.'

Doctor Grechko nods solemnly. 'I'm afraid it is. No matter what you may currently believe, you are Doctor Georgi Kizim. You're even wearing his coat. Look in the pocket if you doubt me—there's a good chance you still have his security pass.'

'No,' I insist. 'I am not Georgi Kizim. I know that man, but I'm not him. I just took his coat, so that I could escape. I am the cosmonaut, Dimitri Ivanov. I was on the *Tereshkova*. I went into the Matryoshka.'

'No,' Doctor Grechko corrects patiently. 'You are not the cosmonaut. He was—is, to a degree—your patient. You were assigned to treat him, to learn what you could. Unfortunately, the protocol was flawed. We thought we could prevent a repeat of what happened with Yakov, the bleed-over of personality and memory, but we were wrong. You began to identify too strongly with your patient, just as Doctor Malyshev began to identify with Yakov. We still don't understand the mechanism, but after the business with Malyshev we thought we'd put in enough safeguards to stop it happening twice. Clearly, we were wrong about that. Even with Ivanov in his vegetative state ...'

'I am Ivanov,' I say, but with a chink of doubt opening inside me.

'Maybe you should look in the coat,' Nesha says.

My fingers numb with cold, I dig into the pocket until I touch the hard edge of his security pass. The hatted man's still keeping a good hold on my arm. I pass the white plastic rectangle to Nesha. She squints, holding it at arm's length, studying the little hologram.

'It's you,' she says. 'There's no doubt.'

I shake my head. 'There's been a mistake. Our files mixed up. I'm not Doctor Kizim. I remember being on that ship, everything that happened.'

'Only because you spent so much time in his presence,' Grechko says, not without compassion. 'After Dimitri fell into the intermittent vegetative state, we considered the risks of contamination to be significantly reduced. We relaxed the safeguards.'

'I am not Doctor Kizim.'

'You'll come out of it, Georgi—trust me. We got Malyshev back in the end. It was traumatic, but eventually his old personality resurfaced. Now he remembers being Yakov, but he's in no doubt as to his core identity. We can do the same for you, I promise. Just come back with us, and all will be well.'

'Look at the picture,' Nesha says, handing the pass back to me.

I do. My eyes take a moment to focus—the snow and the cold are making them water—but when they do there's no real doubt. I'm looking at the same face that I'd seen in the mirror in Nesha's apartment. Cleaned and tidied, but still me.

'I'm scared.'

'Of course you're scared. Who wouldn't be?' Grechko stubs out the cigarette and extends a gloved hand. 'Will you come with us now, Georgi? So that we can start helping you?'

'I have no choice, do I?'

'It's for the best.'

Seeing that I'm going to come without a struggle, Grechko nods at the man with the syringe to put it back in his pocket. The other hatted man gives me an encouraging shove, urging me to start walking along the landing to the waiting elevator. I resist for a moment, looking back at Nesha.

I crave some last moment of connection with the woman I've risked my life to visit.

She nods once.

I don't think Grechko or the other men see her do it. Then she pulls her hand from her pocket and shows me the musical box, before closing her fist on it as if it's the most secret and precious thing in the universe. As if recalling something from a dream, I remember another hand placing that musical box in mine. It's the hand of a cosmonaut, urging me to do something before he slips into coma.

I have no idea what's going to happen to either of us now. Nesha's old, but she could easily have decades of life ahead of her. If she's ever doubted that she was right, she now has concrete proof. A life redeemed, if it needed redeeming. They'll still find every excuse to humiliate her at every turn, given the chance.

But she'll know with an iron certainty they're wrong, and she'll also know that everything they stand for will one day turn to dust.

Small consolation, but you take what you can get.

'Am I really Doctor Kizim?' I ask Grechko, as the elevator takes us down.

'You know it in your heart.'

I stroke my face, measuring it against the memories I feel to be real. 'I was so sure.'

'That's the way it happens. But it's a good sign that you're already questioning these fundamental certainties.'

'The cosmonaut?' I ask, suddenly unable to mention him by name.

'Yes?'

'You mentioned him being in an intermittent vegetative state.'

'He's been like that for a while. I'm surprised you don't remember. He just lies there and watches us. Watches us and hums, making the same tune over and over again. One of us recognised it eventually.' With only mild interest Grechko adds: 'That piece by Prokofiev, the famous one?'

'Troika,' I say, as the door opens. 'Yes, I know it well.'

They take me out into the snow, to the Zil that must have been waiting out of sight. The man with the syringe walks ahead and opens the rear passenger door, beckoning me into it as if I'm some high-ranking party official. I get in without causing a scene. The Zil's warm and plush and silent.

As we speed away from Star City, I press my face against the glass and watch the white world rush by as if in a sleigh-ride.